SINGULARITIVE RANCH

First Contact Last Resort

A Sci Fi Novella 1

First published by Singularitive Ranch 2023

Copyright © 2023 by Singularitive Ranch

All rights reserved. No part of this publication may be reproduced, stored or transmitted in any form or by any means, electronic, mechanical, photocopying, recording, scanning, or otherwise without written permission from the publisher. It is illegal to copy this book, post it to a website, or distribute it by any other means without permission.

This novel is entirely a work of fiction. The names, characters and incidents portrayed in it are the work of the author's imagination. Any resemblance to actual persons, living or dead, events or localities is entirely coincidental.

Singularitive Ranch has no responsibility for the persistence or accuracy of URLs for external or third-party Internet Websites referred to in this publication and does not guarantee that any content on such Websites is, or will remain, accurate or appropriate.

Designations used by organizations to distinguish their products and services are often claimed as trademarks. All brand names and product names used in this book and on its cover are trade names, service marks, trademarks, and registered trademarks of their respective owners. The publisher and the book are not associated with any product or organization mentioned in this book. None of the organizations referenced within the book have endorsed the book.

Tools such as Grammarly and ProWriterAid were used in the editing process, but no generative AI tools were used to compose the story, audiobook, cover art, or marketing materials.

The future scenarios in this speculative fiction series are intended to be thought-provoking, not predictions of the future or aspirations for the future.

First edition

ISBN: 979-8-9879386-0-7

This book was professionally typeset on Reedsy.
Find out more at reedsy.com

Contents

I   Part One

1	Pariah	3
2	The Presentation	5
3	Compulsion	16
4	Rifts	20
5	Slingshot	27
6	Reprimand	29
7	Breakup	34
8	Demarcation	37
9	Date	40
10	Expectations	45
11	Doubt	47
12	Moon	51
13	Risks	53
14	Ambiguity	55
15	Collision	58
16	Rock Climbing	60
17	Rock Stars	63

II Part Two

18	Mentor	69
19	Protest	75
20	Goad	79
21	Threats	85
22	Raid	90
23	Anarchist	96
24	Dissension	99
25	Despondence	106

III Part Three

26	Message	113
27	Surfing	119
28	Knocks	121
29	Singularitive	125
30	More Discoveries	128
31	Sunset	132
32	More Announcements	135
33	Portend	139

Note to Readers — 141

I

Part One

1

Pariah

Seven days. That's how long it had taken Lita to go from rock-star professor to rock-bottom pariah. She curled up in a fetal position, with a scratchy wool blanket pulled over her head, on a stiff mattress in a musty, one-bedroom dwelling. Probably housing for junior officers on a California military base long abandoned. The FBI had sequestered her at the secret location, ten or maybe fifteen hours ago, allegedly for her protection. How long would she have to endure this nightmare, alone and anxious?

She rolled on her back, yanked the blanket off her face, and grimaced at the water stain on the ceiling. Was her life stained forever? Only days ago, she'd had an online citizen-verified poll rating of eighty-one percent and her faculty tenure promotion was certain. Now death threats pummeled her social media feed, and the university had placed her on academic probation. Even worse, Homeland Security's new Free Speech Force was investigating her for distributing fabrications with the intent to disrupt society—minimum sentence: five years.

She flinched when pounding at the front door interrupted

the incessant dripping from the bathroom sink. She got up on her elbows and pursed her lips. Had they come to charge her with breaking the free speech law and take her away in shackles, orphaning her research that could save the planet?

A howling wind ruffled the tattered beige curtains on the window to her side. It was open wide enough for her to squeeze through and escape.

She rubbed her eyes. How had everything gone astray so fast? Maybe there were warning signs during her presentation thirteen days ago she should've heeded.

2

The Presentation

13 Days Earlier
2033 January 14 10:10 AM

* * *

Lita waited offstage, clenched in a power pose with her hands on her hips and shoulders rolled back. She needed to crush this presentation. It could make the difference between attaining her dream tenured faculty position at University of California, Berkeley or finding something else to do with her life. Posing like Wonder Woman boosted her confidence, and she wanted to leverage every advantage she could muster.

She secured her augmented-reality monocle's frame around her ear and flexed her wrist, switching the image in the monocle to a fish-eye view of the auditorium. It rumbled with a standing-room-only audience of about a hundred academics, along with scattered journalists, vloggers, and influencers, whose bright yellow media badges dotted the crowd. Text in the image's corner indicated thousands of others, mostly high school students, were attending online. The university's new requirement that seminars engage the public as well as researchers had plunged her into a week of dithering about her presentation's depth and tone. Thousands of people would judge her performance and possibly influence her tenure decision.

She turned to the stage. At the lectern, the chair of Berkeley's astronomy department cued Lita with a glance and nod. "Please join me in giving a warm welcome to Computational Astrophysics Professor Amelita Bloom."

As polite audience applause greeted her, Lita walked across the stage and stopped at its center, behind a table covered with a blue and gold skirt emblazoned with the UC Berkeley logo. The table held an apple she had placed there earlier. Resuming her Pilates-strong posture, she flashed a smile at the audience, bit off a chunk of the apple, held the fruit in front of her with an extended arm, and let it go—like a mic drop. The apple and table collided, bruising the fruit. Lita chewed, swallowed, and said, "There is gravity, therefore collision."

She paused and searched faces in the audience for expressions indicating she'd charmed them with her theatrical allusion to the legend of Newton's falling apple paired with Descartes' proposition, 'I think, therefore exist.' Her mom had always said that the best educators entertained and inspired people while informing them.

But some attendees were stone-faced. That crushed her delight and stoked her deep-seated fear that the presentation might flop—especially in the eyes of several senior colleagues in her field. They were on the committees for her upcoming tenure promotion and research funding renewal. Had they found her opening flippant? She probably should tone down her theatrics and stick to the facts, even if that bored the high school students watching.

She planted a smile on her face and continued with the introduction to her lab's research. "Around sixty-six million years ago, the Chicxulub asteroid collided with Earth in the Yucatán Peninsula. The resulting mass extinction wiped out seventy-five percent of all plant and animal species—including all non-avian dinosaurs."

Lita stepped behind the steel-topped glass lectern at the side of the stage and launched a holographic projection in the center of the stage. The projection dramatized the Chicxulub collision. The floor-to-ceiling windows in the penthouse auditorium of the seven-story Smoot-Perlmutter Hall darkened and obscured the view of San Francisco and the Golden Gate Bridge.

"Millions of asteroids and comets streak around our solar system. The Tunguska meteor in 1908, Chelyabinsk meteor in 2013, and Edmonton meteor in 2027 were wake-up calls that another significant collision with Earth will happen. It's just a matter of time."

A journalist in the front row raised her hand. Lita pointed at her.

"Is this something we need to worry about in this century, or even millennium?"

"Fair question," Lita said. "Like a pandemic, it seems far away until it's not. But NASA thinks it's a problem. The agency estimates there are over twenty-five thousand near-Earth objects. Those are asteroids and comets that come within two hundred million kilometers of our planet. In 2016, the agency established the Planetary Defense Coordination Office to address this threat."

Lita advanced the presentation to a visualization of planets orbiting the sun as it sped around the center of the galaxy.

"NASA's Near-Earth Object Threat Assessment 2028 Update states, quote, 'Current telescopic and algorithmic-based approaches for detecting Earth collisions cover just a fraction of the sky at any given time, don't provide enough accuracy, and consequently won't give us sufficient warning before impact.'"

She flipped up her monocle over its sleek metal frame. "In comparison, our new technology enables us to chart the paths of thousands of near-Earth objects with a hundred times the accuracy. Our research can identify Earth collisions confidently and with enough warning time to prevent them, using NASA's asteroid deflection technology."

Lita changed the projection to show the logo of NASA's Planetary Defense Coordination Office. "That's my intro to our research. Next, three members of my lab team will highlight their work on this project. But first I want to thank NASA for its steadfast funding—even while we had problems getting the technology to provide consistently accurate results."

Now Lita needed her lab team members to nail their presentations. Their personalities differed and had caused clashes in the lab. Hopefully those conflicts wouldn't be apparent to the audience and show that Lita had struggled to keep her team in line.

Lita nodded at her lab's postdoctoral researcher, sitting front and center of the auditorium. "First up," she said, as the postdoc limped up the three steps to join her on the stage, "is Dr. Marc Romney, our team's expert on neural networks." Lita gave him a reassuring smile.

Marc needed the seminar to go well too. Yesterday, Marc had told her his wife was pregnant, and now he was even more worried about finding a faculty position. Searching for Earth collisions wasn't at the forefront of astrophysics, so Marc's resume didn't stand out.

Marc flipped up his US Marine Corps-issued, augmented-reality monocle and unbuttoned his navy-blue tweed jacket, revealing more of his white Oxford shirt buttoned to his neck. "We achieved our breakthrough in identifying Earth collisions by optimizing a neural network for the latest generation of quantum computers. We call our system 'ECN,' an abbreviation for Earth Collision Neuralnet."

He changed the projection to a flythrough of a diagram depicting ECN's neural net and stepped to the side of the lectern. "Over the past several years, our lab team has trained the neural net on how celestial bodies move in space by feeding it over thirteen years of spatial and attribute data that encompasses every space object larger than fifty kilograms within four light-years of Earth. Augmenting gravitational algorithms with ECN outperforms the algorithm-only approach, because ECN accounts for keyhole, billiard ball, and butterfly effects, and also dynamical chaos."

After Marc had explained how ECN uses its spatial map and corresponding attribute database of over twenty million celestial objects, Lita thanked him and smiled at her grad student, ensconced in the far-left corner of the auditorium. "Next up is our graduate student researcher, Jase Park-Muller, the team's quantum computer guru."

Jase plodded to the stage in his blue and white striped cardigan sweater, khaki pants, and brown loafers. At the lectern he switched the projection to show the lab's quantum computer complex, the size of a city block. "ECN limits its analysis to the fifty-year paths of near-Earth objects at least one hundred forty meters in diameter. That's about the size of a football stadium. Those objects would strike Earth with more energy than the most powerful nuclear device ever tested. So, they'd in-in-inflict severe regional damage."

Lita winced. Jase could get flustered when he stuttered in public.

"How long does it take to determine each object's fifty-year path?" a vlogger asked from the middle of the auditorium.

Jase stuck his hands in his front pockets. "ECN's analysis is massively iterative. Each iteration improves the accuracy of an object's path—as shown on Graph A on the screen. So, ECN produces preliminary fifty-year paths in minutes. But depending on the complexity of an object's gravitational in-interactions, it can take several hours for paths to become precise to the end of the fifty-year timeline."

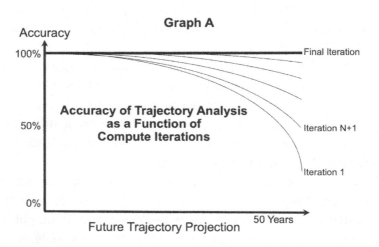

When Jase finished elaborating, Lita waved at the final speaker, the youngest member of her lab. He bounded down to the stage from the back of the room, clad in a Cal-logo hoody, chino shorts, and flip-flops.

"Our last speaker is Rynomo Alqo," Lita said, "our senior undergraduate student researcher and data visualization specialist."

Ryno stood next to the hologram, ran his hand through his neon-blue-dyed hair, and flipped up his aviator-style monocle with a blue tint that matched his blue eyes.

At Berkeley it wasn't surprising for professors to co-present important seminars with their postdocs and grad students. But Lita also liked giving talented undergraduate lab members opportunities to excel. That's why she'd allowed Ryno to co-present. Though now she was having second thoughts. She couldn't do anything about Ryno's hair, and the shorts were okay, but next time she'd advise him to wear shoes. Hopefully he'd be more professional about his presentation.

Ryno advanced the hologram to a visualization of asteroids colliding in the Kuiper Belt. "ECN produces data-intensive reports. Even though the results are prioritized, starting with collisions and flybys, the reports are hard for humans to interpret—except for Jase." Ryno grinned at his lab mate. "To make the reports easier to comprehend, we use holograms to visualize the paths. As shown here, we can see the paths and collisions."

After Ryno finished captivating the audience with his five-minute demo, Lita returned to center stage behind the table. "That's a summary of our research." She picked up the apple and took a nibble-sized bite. "Any questions?"

The audience responded with spirited applause. Lita beamed with the satisfaction of the presentation going smoothly and ending with her allusion to Eve audaciously eating the apple in the Garden of Eden. Maybe some would get the reference to her lab's audacious approach of integrating quantum deep learning with algorithmic computation to search for Earth collisions. When she had proposed that approach, many doubted it would be better than algorithmic methods alone. Some were still skeptical.

Finally, the Q and A session needed to go well. This unscripted part of the seminar was unpredictable. Some in the audience were known for asking tough or unexpected questions—not because they were cruel, but because they were brilliant. Lita sipped from a glass of water, hoping no one noticed her trembling grip.

Professor Mei Jing, sitting stone-faced in the second row, posed the first question. "Your technology is impressive. Why haven't you applied it to other astrophysics research areas?"

"Thanks for that question," Lita said. Mei was on Lita's tenure committee. Was Mei implying that the Earth collision project wasn't worthy academic research, as some had insinuated? Lita bit her lip and recalled her first day of college when her mother had admonished, "Lita, stop with the defeatist imposter syndrome."

"NASA's funding is solely to search for Earth collisions," Lita said. "There are twenty thousand entries in the dataset of near-Earth objects one hundred forty meters and larger. We estimate it'll take a decade to complete the research. Also, we have a sense of urgency because who doesn't want to know about an Earth collision as soon as possible?" She smiled in response to the scattered laughter at her quip, though Mei remained expressionless and folded her arms. "So we haven't used the tech for other applications yet."

Lita scanned the room for other questions. What was Jase doing at the side exit door? His head faced Lita, but his eyes were lowered, jaw slack, eyebrows pinched. He glanced at Lita, turned, and left the auditorium, not bothering to keep the door from slamming shut. Last month Lita had seen the same expression on him, just before he'd disappeared for a week to immerse himself in the Centauri three-star system and three-body problem of orbital physics. Jase's insatiable curiosity could compulsively distract him. Occasionally Lita had to rein him in. Even if the question about using ECN for other applications piqued his interest, Jase should have stayed for the entire Q and A session. Only he could answer some questions about how ECN works. Later she'd have to talk to him about etiquette and her expectations.

A young man attending via the internet-S asked, "If your ECN computer uses machine learning-based pattern recognition in addition to human-written algorithms, then you can't follow how it determines paths. So how can you possibly know that every ECN report is accurate?"

"Great question," Lita said, looking at the back wall of the auditorium that displayed an audio-visual composite of the internet-S attendees. "As part of its reinforcement-learning process, ECN continually compares its reports with subsequent actual movements. After years of training, its reports have maintained a 99.998 percent level of accuracy over the past thirteen months."

Marc stood and faced the audience. "Also, to maintain real-time confidence in ECN's analysis we programmed it to compute past trails of space objects, in addition to their future paths. That enables ECN to instantly compare its results with archives. If there's a discrepancy, we'll know there's a problem. Seoul

University and Penn State researchers originated that rollback technique back in 2021 with their machine-learning generated dark matter map."

After the presentation, Lita lingered on the stage to answer additional questions from a long queue of attendees, her confidence now buoyed—at least for the moment. Also on stage, Marc talked to a visiting professor, probably inquiring about a potential faculty position. Ryno continued doing what he loved—showing off more of his ECN visualization examples.

Most likely, Jase was back at the ECN lab. Hopefully Lita wouldn't need to rein him in again. She had enough challenges to worry about. Her stress was already overwhelming.

Examples of the many styles of AR monocles

3

Compulsion

> Most people assume predicting asteroid collisions,
> especially with enough lead time
> to deflect a collision,
> is ordinary science.
> —Scott Manley (YouTube Rocket Scientist)
> *Why Keyholes Make It So Hard
> to Predict Asteroid Impacts*

* * *

With the necessities of the ECN seminar over, Jase returned to his element, his black metal desk and gray padded chair at the ECN lab in front of the wall-size screen interface to the quantum computer—his throne, his altar, and his cradle. The screen displayed a visualization of ECN's iterating analysis of the near-Earth object, 2020 GA3.

He squinted at the screen but fixated on the question from the morning's seminar about applying ECN to other research areas. The implications inflamed a mental itch that had been vexing him.

When the 2020 GA3 analysis ended, his reflection on the blank screen grabbed his attention. His recently deceased dad appeared to be watching him. Jase's facial features resembled his Korean father, but below the neck he had the physique of his German mom. He was soft, but not overweight, typical of a person who didn't exercise but had a healthy metabolism. He had no time to exercise or, for that matter, socialize. Instead, he emulated the drive of his role model—his workaholic dad. It wasn't like he and his dad were shy or boring. They were just manic about their research, and that crowded out most other activities.

"Sorry I didn't take you to this morning's seminar," he said to his only friend, Cogg. The emotional-support robot sat like a lioness on the floor, eyeing Jase. "Pets aren't allowed in that new au-auditorium, even furry-faced machines."

The realistic-looking cross between a cat and mid-size dog purred and panted as if the AI-imbued robot accepted Jase's apology.

Jase stroked Cogg's thick calico fur and refocused on the question about other ways to apply the ECN tech. That was one of the questions he'd been asking himself over the past few weeks. The technology that he'd created along with his lab colleagues had so many possibilities. They weren't taking advantage of its full potential.

Lately he'd ruminated that discovering a pending Earth collision or even a scientifically significant flyby might take years—and probably beyond his PhD time in this lab. Was he destined to be like his dad, brilliant but toiling in obscurity, then dying suddenly?

"Maybe," he muttered to Cogg, "brief little ECN experiments

might lead to discovering something soon." Cogg's ears perked up.

Jase leaned back in his chair and turned to the window. The quad outside bustled with students walking to their classes. The campus's campanile gonged, announcing eleven o'clock. He had lots of ideas for side experiments. For example, what would ECN report if he directed it at the nearest star system?

His curiosity snowballed into an obsession. Should he discuss this with the team first? Now that they'd completed the engrossing development of the ECN technology, the search process had become tedious. He wanted new challenges. The other lab members were probably having the same thoughts.

He smiled at Cogg and shook his head. "Nah, no need to wait." He swiveled in his chair back to his screen and opened an ECN program he'd been working on intermittently. Over the next fifty minutes, he modified the program to redirect ten percent of ECN's enormous computing capacity away from near-Earth object analyses and targeted it at Centauri—the star system closest to the sun.

After setting up the experiment, he glanced at the wall clock. If he didn't leave for his class within a minute, he'd be late. He hated walking in late in front of the professor and his classmates. The classroom image reminded him to take his stutter medicine. Just a half dose. The full dose gave him headaches.

Should he launch the experiment or think about it more? He took a deep breath, reached down to hold Cogg's head with both hands, and studied its facial expression. With its ears down, Cogg seemed to be conveying, *It's wrong to steal computing time. The lab team might stop trusting you. This could get you kicked out of your PhD program.*

"No way," Jase said. "Berkeley students have a tradition of

skimming computing time for their side projects and startups. And if the funding committee discovers this brief diversion, I'll just ask for forgiveness. The campus celebrates maverick scientists—who didn't ask permission."

With that final reasoning, Jase gave the oral command "ECN, launch Centauri an-analysis" and hurried to his class, wondering if his side experiment would turn up anything interesting.

4

Rifts

Having stayed late at her ECN seminar to answer numerous questions, Lita power-walked along the Berkeley campus's Strawberry Creek to get to her lunch meeting on time. Her triad of brunette ponytails—one over each ear and the third just behind the crown of her head—bounced with each stride of the white slipper-sneakers that carried her trim frame.

Though she wanted to be on time for the meeting, she had doubts about its value. The topic had nothing to do with her research or getting her tenure promotion.

As she entered a shabby classroom in the basement of Campbell Hall, a middle-aged woman at the front of the room flipped up her monocle over its 2020s retro-styled frame and said to the fifteen assembled people, "We'll get started in a minute."

Lita scanned the room of unfamiliar faces, spotted her best friend, Benna, and sat beside her. The two exchanged smiles and mouthed hellos. Benna added a nod and a thumbs-up. She had urged Lita to come to this meeting, claiming that geopolitical insights would help Lita navigate the politics of the campus, and life.

Lita was skeptical. She was drawn to subjects that influenced her daily life or she could use to influence the world. In kindergarten she became fascinated by the moon after her mom explained how its orbit influenced the tides along her Long Island coastal town. In high school she immersed herself in machine learning after discovering how she could use it to address hard problems. Geopolitics was a distant subject, and this meeting would probably be an unproductive waste of her time. But not wanting to ignore her friend's advice, Lita pulled a lunch bag out of her backpack and settled in to listen to the woman poised to start the meeting.

"I'm Roberta Sanchez, the inaugural president of the Berkeley chapter of the UMS3—the Union for the Mitigation of Societal Stratification and Strife—an offshoot of the Union of Concerned Scientists. Welcome to the second monthly meeting of our chapter. Nice to see several new faces. For those of you who missed our first meeting, I'll recap who we are, then discuss our plans for the Berkeley chapter."

The president walked to the middle of the room, surrounded by the attendees at desks arranged in a circle. "The union is a new organization of higher ed students, faculty, and staff who're concerned that too many communities are becoming mostly populated by residents with an identical and uncompromising cultural mindset—related to politics, religion, or lifestyles. Research shows that this epidemic of geo-psychographic stratification, GPS, is increasing strife between communities that could lead to civil war. We aim to study ways to blunt this sorting of mindsets and the resulting cultural fiefdoms."

The president took a gulp from her hydration bottle, and Lita checked the time. Maybe she wouldn't need to stay for the entire session to satisfy Benna.

"Here's our union's premise," the president said. "Over eons, humans have evolved to form groups whose members share traits. But a trend that skyrocketed in the early twenty-first century has caused an anti-social overexpression of this adaptation."

She advanced her presentation to the next slide. "The trend is the ubiquity of websites such as YourPeople.info that have drawn folks, like never before, to communities with high concentrations of residents with a particular mindset. Put simply, everyone knows where to find and live with like-minded people."

The president pointed to a graph on the slide. "Accelerating that trend is the first law of geo-psychographics, which states that the rate of separation increases as the degree of concentration increases. In other words, the greater the concentrations, the stronger the attraction. Interestingly, this law is applicable to the metaverse as well as our physical world."

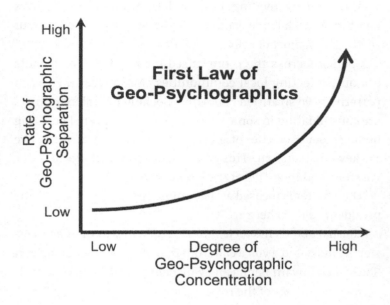

Benna's hand shot up. The president nodded at her. Benna stood and tucked her crimson hair behind her ears. "Hi everyone. I'm Benna Herst, a professor of social epidemiology in Berkeley's School of Public Health. My research shows that an additional dynamic causing this problem is a new strain of online influencers who promote homogeneous towns as utopias. They're persuading people not to want to live among or have anything to do with folks who have differing views. They're also offering financial incentives."

The president continued nodding. "Yes, I've read your papers. Those utopian memes have worsened the stratification. Many of the memes are baseless. And most of those influencers make their income by dividing us. I think US Homeland Security's new Free Speech Force needs to do a better job of enforcing our DF-DS law against distributing fabrications to disrupt society."

A person across the room raised his hand. "This trend's not only affecting local communities. Multi-year migration patterns have stratified countries. Socially liberal extremists are consolidating in some nations, while others are becoming homogeneous societies of socially conservative extremists, like Turkey and Pakistan. This could cleave the Civil World order. We should address GPS at the global scale too."

"Our charter is focused at the community level in the US," the president said. "There are NGOs—"

A flash on Lita's monocle interrupted her focus on the discussion. It indicated a voice call from Dan Malcolm, her boyfriend. She leaned toward Benna and whispered, "Back in a minute."

Lita stepped out of the room. "Hey, Danno, what's up?"

"Hi. Just want to remind you about our dinner date at six."

"Oh yeah, looking forward to it."

"I watched your seminar. You rocked."

"Yep, my team nailed it."

"I have a good feeling about your tenure promotion."

"I don't know. I think we convinced the audience that developing ECN was world-class research. But I still wonder if some faculty think the collision search should be done at NASA, not a research university."

"Lita, there's always naysayers. Stop with the imposter syndrome."

A notice flashed on Lita's monocle. "Oh, I just got a reminder. I'm teaching in thirty minutes. I need to review my lecture notes. See you at dinner."

After the call, Lita opened her online calendar. She needed to be more diligent about scheduling social events. Wait, did Dan say six or seven o'clock? She'd have to worry about that later.

She turned to walk down the hallway, then looked back through the window in the door where the union meeting was continuing. The geopolitical discussion was more interesting than she'd expected. It'd be nice to stay for the entire meeting. Later, she'd thank Benna for the suggestion.

Now she needed to access her lecture notes and get to her class on time. Today's topic was the n-body problem in gravitational physics. If she wasn't fully prepared, she'd struggle not only to teach the complex topic but, equally importantly, to enthuse her students.

Lita paused at the top of Campbell Hall's steps overlooking its plaza. Like celestial bodies in a solar system, a jumble of Berkeley students animated the plaza, a mix of order and apparent disorder. She rubbed her chin. Interestingly, the union's discussion had analogies to the n-body problem of predicting the gravitational interactions and trajectories of more than three celestial bodies in a group. Similar to mass in gravitational physics, the greater the geo-concentration of mindsets, the stronger the attraction of people to those mindsets. Also, as with celestial bodies, the dynamic interactions of more than three geo-psychographic mindsets made it hard to predict the trajectory of those mindsets and the world as a whole.

Lita strode through the plaza and onto her class, her eyes fixed on the pavement. The analogous patterns had a certain beauty. Yet there were differences. To stem social strife, the union intended to determine ways to influence mindsets. Astrophysicists had no illusions of affecting a group of celestial bodies. Though, it'd be fascinating to have that capability.

Lita touched the side of her monocle and added the union's

meeting schedule to her calendar. Was it hubris to try to predict and influence the trajectory of the world? She'd find out.

5

Slingshot

After his class and lunch, Jase returned to the ECN lab with Cogg in tow. Back in his chair in front of the screen, he opened ECN's first preliminary report of Centauri, and browsed through the numbers.

The report's data came to life in his mind's eye. He jerked forward. "Fascinating." One enormous celestial body arching toward another large celestial body. He looked at Cogg. "A natural gravitational slingshot. Could that be possible?" Cogg tilted its head sideways.

He studied the report for a minute, then d-messaged the lab team.

= *This morning's seminar question about using ecn for other apps obsessed me. So i launched a mini experiment by redirecting 10% of ecn at the centauri star system. Check out the attached prelim report.*

While he waited for a response, Jase powered up the holographic visualization of ECN's report. He rarely used the visualization capability that Ryno had developed. He had nothing against Ryno's work in the lab, but the visualizations were theatrics for novices and insufficiently detailed for experts. Still, it'd be good to confirm his interpretation of the raw data.

A d-message from Lita interrupted him.

= *Jase, you shouldn't redirect ECN without conferring with me & team. Let's meet at 4:30 at the bear's lair to clarify our lab protocols and return 100% of ECN to our mission.*

Jase scratched his head. That was it? Had any of the team even looked at the preliminary report?

Lita d-messaged again.

= *Just now opened the report. The results are intriguing. Let's also discuss at 4:30.*

Jase turned back to the visualization and smiled. It confirmed his interpretation. It could be a natural stellar gravitational slingshot. An astrophysical phenomenon that would inspire his research.

He leaned back in his chair and clasped his hands behind his head, looking forward to the praise Lita and his lab mates would bestow on him. He wasn't going to end up like his dad, lost in history. Too bad his dad hadn't lived long enough to see this. He'd be impressed with his son, finally.

6

Reprimand

First of the lab team to arrive at the Bear's Lair pub, Jase sat under a large umbrella at an outdoor picnic table at the far corner of the courtyard. The distance and din of the crowd would keep the lab team's upcoming conversation confidential. He scratched Cogg's wolf-like erect ears. Cogg performed its soothing combination of purring and panting. The scent of stale beer didn't bother it. Around the corner at Lower Sproul Plaza, the Cal Marching Band practiced "Fight for California."

To Jase's left, a robot waiter audio'd, ^Come on in, Rynomo. Have a seat. Nice to see you again.^

Ryno marched onto the patio in sync with the Cal Band. "Great to be back. We'll start with a pitcher of the house hard cider."

Ryno greeted Jase by wrapping his fisted left hand in the palm of his right hand.

Jase mirrored the gong-shou greeting.

Ryno sat across from Jase and ran his hand through his hair.

Cogg padded over to Ryno and acknowledged him with what looked like a smile along with a bark and eye wink.

Ryno grinned at Cogg and said, "Roll over."

Cogg effortlessly did an acrobatic 360-degree flip and pawed a high five.

"I gotta get one of these," Ryno said. "You need a doctor's prescription to get one, right?"

"Indeed. Some AI experts worry these comfort robots are too experimental and potentially dangerous. But when my dad died a few months ago, my mom convinced our family doc to prescribe the robot. I'm an only child. She thinks I need em- emotional and social support."

"Do you?" Ryno asked.

Just as Jase started to haltingly answer, Lita and Marc arrived from different directions.

Lita sat and lifted her monocle's frame off her ear. "Please flip up your monocles, I want your full attention."

The team members complied—except Jase. He didn't have one.

Marc slammed the table. "Who gave you fricking permission to redirect ECN?"

"You're angry? I expected you to congratulate me for using our tech to make a big discovery."

"What discovery?" Ryno asked. "I haven't opened the report yet."

"The report tentatively in-indicates," Jase said, "that the Proxima Centauri solar system and our solar system are on trajectories that'll put the two systems within 99 to 490 AUs of each other in 102 to 351 years. If the actual results are in the low end of that distance, then from a galactic perspective that's an amazing flyby."

"Wow-ser," Ryno said. "If it's a flyby, why hasn't conventional astronomy forecasted it?"

"ECN's analysis shows Proxima Centauri undergoing a gravitational slingshot with the binary star couple in its three-star system, Alpha Centauri A and B," Jase said. "Gravitational slingshots within star clusters have been hypothesized. Some astrophysicists think that stellar streams are formed by slingshots. This would be the first observation of the phenomenon."

"The analysis is far from definitive yet," Marc said. "A flyby is too improbable. This is nothing more than the two stars nearing each other. But even at their closest, they'll still be astronomically far apart, and consequently of little scientific significance."

Marc narrowed his gray eyes, jutted his square jaw, and pointed his thick index finger at Jase. "This is a damn waste of ECN time. You're slowing our research. Even worse, you're jeopardizing our funding."

Jase reeled back and placed his hand on Cogg's back. This wasn't the first time Marc had bullied him—getting right in his face. He looked at Lita. Why had she never reprimanded Marc? Maybe that had something to do with Marc's research acumen, or his Purple Heart. It couldn't be that she agreed with his sentiments.

Lita took an audible deep breath. The group turned to her. Her head lowered and bobbed. "Marc, I agree. We shouldn't get excited by the early report. And we can't misuse our funding."

She turned to Jase. His chest stiffened, as he anticipated her telling him to stop the side experiment. Her lips turned up. "But sometimes we should take calculated risks. Explore our curiosities. Jase, let ECN continue its Proxima analysis. We'll know within twenty-four hours whether the proximity will be scientifically significant."

Jase nodded and beamed at Cogg, hoping for a facial expression showing praise for the success of their little misappropriation of the computer. Instead Cogg tilted its head down, flattened its ears, and looked at Jase with wide disapproving eyes.

Jase didn't make eye contact with Marc. Even a glance could be perceived as gloating that Lita had prioritized his hunch over Marc's mission focus. Lita had spoken to Jase about team camaraderie. He'd been trying harder to fit in.

After the team had discussed other aspects of the ECN report for a half hour, Lita said, "Two more things. First, I'll ask the multi-spectrum telescope lab at UT Austin to take a close look at Proxima. They recently powered on enhancements to their space telescope that uses the moon as a sun shield. Maybe the telescope can see the slingshot phenomenon emerging. The head of that lab, Luke Johnson, is an old friend. We can trust him. Which leads to my second point."

She briefly made eye contact with Marc and Jase then held her gaze on Ryno. "Aside from Luke, let's keep this tentative report to ourselves. We don't want to start rumors that need to be retracted and hurt our credibility. Everyone with me?"

The team members nodded.

* * *

As Ryno signaled the r-aiter for another pitcher, Lita put her monocle back on. It flashed that she was predicted to be late for her dinner date. With her monocle removed, she'd missed the reminder. Another flash showed that she had fourteen minutes before the next cross-bay hydrofoil ferry departed.

"I gotta run," she said to the group. "I have a dinner

reservation."

She jostled through the crowd at the front of the pub, stepped into an autonomous mini-taxi parked alongside the pub, and rode it to the Berkeley Marina Transit Center. Then she raced down the pier and caught the eleven-minute hydrofoil ferry across the bay to San Francisco.

Lita found a seat on the outdoor upper deck. Her monocle predicted she'd arrive fifteen minutes late. Maybe she could make up some time by sprinting from the dock to the nearby restaurant. Hopefully Dan would forgive her. She connected her tracker to him so at least he could see she was on her way.

While Lita's heaving lungs filled with salty air, a concern welled up in her brain. She admired Jase's curiosity, but worried about his social immaturity. She also worried about Marc's emotional intelligence and confrontational style. Marc and Jase had clashed several times. There was no telling how volatile it would get if Jase's experiment disrupted the lab's funding and momentum, along with Marc's prospects for securing a faculty position to support his young family. Had she made the right decision to continue the side experiment? Did Marc and her department's faculty think she was an incompetent lab manager?

As the ferry skimmed by Treasure Island and her breathing normalized, anxiety over the potential team dissension gave way to wonderment. Would ECN's definitive report reveal a flyby close enough to be a big discovery—the kind that would catapult her career?

7

Breakup

Done with his second mug of cider at the Bear's Lair pub, Ryno pedaled his hybrid electric bike to his apartment in Berkeley's Panoramic Hill neighborhood. His bike seat tilted in its yoke as he leaned into each curve. With his cider buzz, he enjoyed the ride even more than usual. When the Simon and Garfunkel song "Homeward Bound" playing through his monocle got to its chorus, he stood on the pedals and belted out along. He loved twentieth-century rock music.

Ryno coasted down his driveway, entered his apartment's narrow stone foyer, walked into the cramped kitchen, and greeted his girlfriend, Pari Meegat, with a boisterous kiss and hug, lifting her clean off the ground.

He opened the fridge and poured cider into his favorite beer stein to continue his celebration. Golden liquid sloshed over the top. He couldn't help himself from counting his chickens before they hatched. The potential discovery made his head buzz, even more than the alcohol.

"House, start my Celebratory Playlist," he said. Kool and the Gang's "Celebration" rocked over the apartment's speakers.

"House, decrease volume to background level," Pari shouted and pointed at the cider. "That's why my father wants me to end our relationship. You're partying at six o'clock instead of studying. Is that what you Alberta farm boys do after a day of baling hay?"

"That's no different from you Kuala Lumpur big city girls hitting those fancy bars after an afternoon of shopping." He took a gulp and raised his mug as if toasting. "Besides, I don't have to study anymore. I'm now part of a future Nobel Prize-winning team. We might even get considered for a Singularitive Prize. What global award has your dad won, City Girl?"

"At best, you might be part of an Ig Nobel Prize-winning team, Farm Boy."

"Is being on the team that discovered that the Proxima solar system and our solar system are gonna fly by each other Nobel or Ig Nobel?" He let the secret escape his mouth without thinking. He wanted to impress Pari. So he didn't qualify his boast by mentioning that the flyby was only in the range of possible results in ECN's early analysis.

"Okay-uh... sounds bizarre. Let's discuss it later. I'm meeting my dad for dinner in a few minutes. Back at about nine."

Pari flipped down her monocle on its Borg-styled frame, which partially obscured her green left eye. Ryno loved how it made her look like Seven of Nine. He was a big fan of the twentieth-century TV series *Star Trek*.

While American Authors' song "Best Day of My Life" played in the background, Ryno stood at his apartment's large picture window and watched his curvaceous girlfriend's raven-black hair catch the wind as she scootered down the street. If he couldn't keep the flyby secret for more than an hour, could the other lab members, and now Pari, keep it confidential? Wait, did he forget to tell Pari not to tell anyone else about the discovery?

When she was out of sight, he guzzled his remaining cider, and his concern about the secret faded as his other concern sharpened. Would this be the evening that Pari's father convinced her to break up with him?

＃ 8

Demarcation

After the ECN team meeting, Jase walked back to the lab via UC Berkeley's Sproul Plaza. Cogg followed him.

Across the street, a woman strolled with her pit bull mixed breed. The dog tugged at its leash and aggressively barked at Cogg. In anticipation that the dog's behavior might trigger Cogg's bully-defense mode, Jase made sure its collar glowed red.

Cogg glared at the dog and emitted a bark with the resonance of a foghorn and the decibel level of a freight train. That bark sent the pit bull and the dog's owner scurrying away.

The baritone bark drew the attention of a couple walking behind Jase. One of them said to the other, "Wonder what else that thing can do?"

"Don't know, but it's not even on a leash."

Jase paused and prepared to explain to them, *When Cogg's collar is red, it's on a virtual leash that keeps it within five feet of me.* But instead, he shrugged and walked on.

Jase continued to Sproul Plaza and past the seal embedded in the historic square's center that marked the birthplace of the nineteen-sixties' free speech movement. The plaza teemed with hundreds of people assembled in front of Sproul Hall. The smell of cannabis wafted across the plaza.

The leader of the rally ascended the granite steps leading to Sproul Hall, a large neoclassical edifice. When he reached the microphone stand four steps above the plaza, the frumpy man with shoulder-length gray hair turned towards the crowd. "I'm Bernie Shasta, mayor of the City of Berkeley and proud member of the Muwekma Ohlone Tribe. It's heartening to see so many people here to protest yesterday's news. Hackers uncovered a confidential document on the Consortium of the Civil World's servers. It revealed that thirty percent of humanity in the A-civil World—we're talking over a billion people—live in conditions comparable to medieval times."

The crowd shouted in shared anger. Jase paused and did a half-hearted fist pump. The speech didn't rile him, but he didn't want to stand out. These social causes didn't interest him. He wanted to get back to the ECN lab.

But when he took a step to continue to the lab, Cogg sat, turned its ears forward, and watched the mayor. Surprised, but not annoyed, Jase remained by Cogg. During his comfort robot's orientation class, he had learned it was programmed to act in ways it thought would help Jase, and that help might be subtle or unexpected. That was, in part, why he went from his initial doubts about having the robot to delight with his pet. Now he was curious about Cogg's behavior, not the mayor's speech, but he listened nonetheless.

"Everyone acknowledges," the mayor said, "that prior to the demarcation of our planet's geography and corresponding population into two zones, the Civ World and the A-civ World, warlords in failed states fueled terrorism and refugee calamities.

We all also acknowledge that electronically walling off the warlord regions halted those problems—but only for us, not them."

The mayor raised his hands. "Turning our backs on billions of innocent people in the A-civ World is appalling. Especially because some of the refugee crisis resulted from sea-level rise, largely caused by the affluent nations that divided the world and established the Consortium."

The protesters booed and hissed at the mention of "The Consortium." Jase booed too. The mob's emotion was contagious. Cogg glanced at him, quizzically tilted its head to the side, and returned its focus to the mayor.

"We're not demanding a return to the days of military intervention. That failed. Instead, we believe small acts of aid can improve the plight of billions of people. That's the goal of our Human Welfare Initiative."

The mayor pointed south toward Telegraph Avenue. "Let's now march to our new People's Park Memorial to let our nation's leaders know how we, the people, feel."

The protesters marched loudly but peacefully toward the memorial.

Jase padded Cogg's head. "That was more interesting than expected. Nice diversion." He turned in the same direction as the march and led Cogg toward the ECN lab.

9

Date

On the outdoor deck of Sam's Anchor Bistro, Dan sipped a glass of New Zealand sauvignon blanc and rehashed what he planned to say to Lita during dinner. Sailboats glided on the bay in front of Alcatraz Island. Seagulls squawked overhead.

He checked his plain-styled monocle for an update on Lita's location. Over the four years he'd been dating Lita, he'd come to expect her to be punctual for professional events but often late for social occasions. She wasn't rude, just focused on her work, and that sidetracked her attention to social matters. For this latest tardiness, at least she had shown some contriteness by linking her position tracker so he could monitor her progress. That was why, when she trotted toward the table, he didn't prepare to complain. Instead, he took off his monocle frame, kissed her cheek, and pointed to the glass of Paso Robles zinfandel, waiting for her.

"Cheers," Dan said.

"To star... dust and stardust," Lita said, raising her glass. "So sorry I'm late."

"Quite all right. How was your afternoon?"

"Oh, we have an interesting analysis running on ECN. That's what held me up."

"A potential collision?"

"No, maybe an anomaly. It's too preliminary to discuss." She wiped her forehead. "What about your day?"

"Aside from teaching and research, I pondered our future."

She took a sip of wine. "Hmm, tell me more."

"I will, but first let's order dinner. I already have a bowl of your favorite Tomales Bay mussels coming."

Dan ordered via the table's interface to the kitchen. While browsing the wine menu to choose his second glass, he looked up to ask Lita if she remembered whether 2026 was a wildfire year for Napa wines. But Lita had flipped down her monocle, a breach of etiquette that stifled his question.

"Danno, I'm going to the bathroom to wash the ferry ride off my hands and face," she said, with her monocle still engaged.

Alone again, Dan bowed his head. He'd come to accept that Lita would often arrive late, but it was rude for her to use her monocle during their date. Maybe this dinner wasn't the right time for his surprise. Maybe there'd never be a right time for Lita.

Minutes later, she returned to a table full of food and flipped up her monocle as she sat.

"Food's getting cold," Dan said, raising his bushy left eyebrow. "Let's eat." Though annoyed, he didn't ask about her behavior. Dwelling on it would upset their dinner rapport and risk ruining his surprise.

Before launching into his speech, Dan let Lita settle into the dinner and finish her first glass of wine. She usually needed at least one glass to transition from her serious work mode into an easygoing social mood.

After her second glass of wine had arrived, he leaned across the table and placed his hands on hers. "We've been happily living together for two years. We're climbing and scuba partners. We love sunsets." He pointed across the bay at the silhouette of Mount Tam along the reddening northwestern horizon. "That's almost as beautiful as the boiling sunset we saw on the Lair's Gargoyles hike. Remember that?"

She nodded and smiled, her watery eyes glistening.

He paused, hoping for more of a reaction. Maybe her reminiscing.

Enough setup. Now or never. "Anyway, I think that all shows we're ready to commit. I love you. Amelita Bloom. Will you marry me?"

"Oh Danno, yes. Nothing in the universe would make me happier." She leaped up and hugged him. "You're my soulmate. The love of my life."

He kissed and held his new fiancée for a long moment, ecstatic that his proposal had delighted her.

"I have something for you," he said and pulled a small bamboo box out of his backpack. He opened the box and presented it to Lita. It held a set of synthetic bioluminescent jewelry—earrings, a ring, bracelet, necklace, and hair brooch. He gave the box a shake, causing the jewelry to glow a range of blue to green neon.

"They're beautiful." Her face lit up. "I love 'em." A tear rolled down her cheek.

He put the ring on her left ring finger. She put the brooch in her hair.

During the rest of the dinner, Lita's excitement faded. She became unusually quiet and distant.

Dan took his academic research seriously, but not himself. That's why he walked with a hunch, wore unassuming clothes, and left his curly black hair unruly. The Cape Town surfer vibe he was raised on made it easy for him to shrug off Lita's tepid behavior with subtle humor. "It's nice to see our engagement's having such a calming effect on you," he said and raised his eyebrow again.

After dinner, he led the way out of the crowded restaurant. She intertwined their arms and squeezed his hand. Despite her distractedness, the engagement dinner's success thrilled him. So did the prospect of a romantic evening.

* * *

Dan chose a scenic route along the waterfront to walk with Lita to their condo. A cleaning robot passed them on the spotless path enclosed in a security fence. The briny bay air mixed with the sweet scent of white and pink flowers of the plum trees that dotted the path's city side.

When they reached a viewpoint, Dan slipped his finger-ring camera on the lookout's cylindrical selfie appendage and took a minute to adjust the camera's settings for the perfect photo to memorialize their engagement evening.

Lita flipped down her monocle.

After getting the angle, shutter speed, and aperture just right, he stepped next to Lita, put his arm around her shoulders, and whispered, "Is something urgent?"

The camera snapped with her monocle flipped down.

He frowned. "Should we take another?"

"Danno, I'm so sorry about my monocle." She rubbed her forehead. "I mentioned we have an ECN analysis underway that could be interesting. I've been checking for updates."

He looked away from her, out to the bay.

Lita gently brought his face back to her. "Marrying you would make me the happiest woman in the cosmos." She pulled off her monocle, pressed his hand against her waist, stood on her toes, and whispered into his ear.

His cheeks warmed from blushing.

10

Expectations

With the San Francisco skyline twinkling through the bedroom window of the twenty-fifth-story condo, Lita stood beside the king size bed, poised to take off her oversized nightshirt and slip under the flannel covers with Dan. But it had been over an hour since she had last checked for an ECN update. The uncertainty would be too distracting for her to enjoy sleeping with Dan.

"I'm so sorry, I have to check ECN one more time."

Dan groaned. "So much for having a romantic engagement evening."

"Okay, okay. I need to tell you what's going on. You'll get why I'm distracted."

Upon hearing about the possible flyby, Dan leaped out of bed, put on his robe, and paced with his arms folded. "How does asteroid collision research lead to a star flyby discovery?"

"A combination of serendipity, curiosity, and impulsiveness. A question during this morning's seminar intrigued Jase. His curiosity morphed into his impulsive decision to redirect ECN at the nearest star system."

"Interesting. A classic case of intuitively brilliant science."

"And intuitive insubordination. If he'd waited to ask the lab team and me for permission, I'm sure we would have said no."

"How do you plan to announce this discovery?"

"Wait. Slow down. We're still not sure this is significant. That's why I keep checking ECN's status."

"I can see the astrophysical significance of a flyby. But, putting on my anthropologist hat, my first thought is, could this affect the planet and our species?"

Before Lita could answer, he leaned forward. "If ECN reveals a near flyby, you shouldn't publicly announce the discovery until it's determined whether the flyby will have a cataclysmic impact on Earth. Maybe it'll change our orbit in a way that causes us to freeze. Or something crazy like cause the moon to collide with Earth."

She chuckled. "I have a good feel for gravitational physics. There's no way this would cataclysmically affect us."

"Sometimes outcomes defy scientific expectations and intuition."

Lita nodded. "That's true. You're right. If this is a flyby, we won't announce it until we determine if there'd be any minor effects. Besides, apocalyptic misinformation would mar our discovery."

While Dan continued speculating about a flyby's implications, Lita sat at the edge of the bed, leaned back on her hands, and swooned over how lucky she was to have found Dan. He shared her fascination with science. He forgave her for being late and distracted. He was her best friend, lover, and now fiancé. Her ECN update could wait. Instead, she pulled her nightshirt over her head and tossed it on the floor, untied and dropped his robe, then led him back to their bed.

11

Doubt

next day
day 2

* * *

Seconds after the ECN lab's wall clock beeped, signaling the arrival of 8:00 a.m., the lab's thick metal door opened and closed with a clang. Jase didn't look up from his chair to greet whoever had entered the lab. He couldn't take his eyes off the ECN feed. Every second a new iteration narrowed the range of the trajectory analysis.

"Morning Jase," Ryno said. "You been here all night?"

"No, just an hour," Jase said, still not looking up.

"You watching ECN's real-time feed?"

"Indeed," Jase said. "When you get good at interpreting the raw feed, it's like watching a high-speed baseball game. The feed is mostly balls and strikes, but every once in a while I get a rush from seeing hits, and someday a home run."

"Good morning, team," Lita said, entering the lab a moment

after Marc had slipped in without a peep. "Jase, my most recent update showed ECN's analysis narrowing, although still not asymptotic. What's the real-time visualization showing?"

Jase turned on the visualization. "The latest but still not final report in-indicates that Proxima and the sun will be nearest to each other in 99 to 156 years. At that time, the stars will be 103 to 127 AUs apart."

Lita and Marc studied the visualization, Lita wide-eyed and open-mouthed, Marc narrow-eyed with downturned lips.

Ryno pointed at himself. "Explain to this comp-sci major whether that's astronomically near or far away."

"That's about three times the distance between the sun and Neptune," Jase said. "It's about half a light-day. From a galactic perspective it's phenomenally close."

Ryno ran his hand through his hair, clapped, and muttered, "Can't wait to tell my girlfriend. Then her father."

Lita frowned at Ryno.

"Of course, not till we're ready to tell people," Ryno said.

Lita turned back to the visualization and shook her head. "Astounding."

Marc nodded and held his chin.

Jase pointed at the ECN screen. "I did a secondary an-analysis. A flyby at 103 AUs, the nearest in ECN's latest report, will cause Earth's orbital distance from our sun to increase by about 1.34 percent. Or, more precisely, between one million and three million kilometers, depending on where Earth and the other planets are in their orbits relative to the sun and Proxima."

Jase looked at Ryno. "That's a small increase, given that Earth's elliptical orbit around the sun currently varies by about six million kilometers."

Ryno raised his hand. "I'm no astrophysicist. I'm just the

software visualization guy here. But how do we know ECN's training on asteroids and comets applies to stars and solar systems?"

"That's the power and beauty of the neural net's machine learning," Jase said. "All celestial bodies are subject to the same gravitational dynamics. That's why I thought this experiment would be interesting. Though I thought maybe ECN would identify a pending collision in the other solar system, not this flyby."

Lita sat in her chair and leaned forward. "Team, this is big. Really big. We need to think carefully about next steps. Before announcing anything, we should be confident about ECN's report."

"Why would we doubt ECN?" Jase asked. "Its reports have been accurate for over a year."

"Right," Lita said. "Still, I'll check back with Luke's lab in Texas. Maybe they've made some progress with their updated space telescope." She pursed her lips. "Also, we should get a better sense of whether the flyby's gravitational effects will affect Earth's biosphere."

"A 1.34 percent change in orbital wobble," Jase said. "That's relatively minor."

"Agreed," Lita said. "But I'd like to have a research-based understanding. Not an intuitive one."

The group discussed how they'd make this assessment on biosphere impact. They concluded that they needed expert help with the climate modeling, especially because they wanted to expedite the analysis. Lita scheduled a meeting with Dr. Lain Gur, a climatologist expert she knew at Lawrence Berkeley National Lab.

Just before the discussion ended, Marc said, "We also need to think about how the flyby's gravitational forces will affect the planets, especially Jupiter. It could also have some billiard ball effects in the asteroid belt."

Jase nodded. Marc was brilliant but still a bully.

12

Moon

next day
day 3

* * *

Lita caught up on her d-message inbox while the autonomous shuttle drove along Cyclotron Road, carrying Jase and her up the green grassy hill between the university and the national lab. She and Jase used the shuttle's onboard DNA scanner to bypass the line of visitors at the national lab's security gate. The lab security prohibited pets and robot visitors, so Jase's cogg idled in his apartment.

Lita led the way into Building 74, the lab's headquarters for the Earth and Environmental Sciences Division. Lain Gur, a pot-bellied, purple-pigtailed, middle-aged climatologist shuffled into the lobby. Lita greeted him, introduced Jase, and followed Lain to his office, jam-packed with books and papers.

Jase presented the flyby data, showed the visualization on Lain's steampunk-styled monocle, and posed the question about the biosphere impact.

"Can you help us?" Lita asked.

"Fascinating," Lain said. "Of course. This is the astro-discovery of the century. And your timing's great. Yesterday we published our research on potential unintended consequences of the Earth-scale engineering plan to cool the planet. It was quite a feat to model the cooling effects of pumping sulfur dioxide into the atmosphere."

Lita's monocle automatically flashed a link to information about Lain's controversial analysis of the proposed SO_2 Earth-scale project. She didn't click the link. She wanted to stay focused on the flyby impact.

"It'll probably take us four to six weeks to complete the Proxima analysis," Lain said.

"Why so long?" Jase asked.

"The modeling is complex. Then there's the moon."

Lita wanted to probe Lain's comment about the moon, but the loquacious climatologist launched into a monologue about how his lab's research had shown that the massive SO_2 project should be effective and safe.

Lain ended the meeting abruptly when he realized he was late for another meeting. "Also, I promise to keep your flyby discovery confidential," he said and hurried away. "At least as long as you can."

Walking back to the shuttle, Jase said to Lita, "I wanted to ask him what his analysis had to do with the moon, but I couldn't get a word in."

"I wondered the same thing. He's a big talker. Like a lot of great scientists. Let's hope he follows through as promised."

13

Risks

evening of the same day

* * *

In her condo's combined kitchen-dining room, adorned with the latest shiny steel-clad appliances, Lita sat down at the glass table. Through the wall of windows to her side, fingers of white fog crept over San Francisco's western hills. "We met with a climatologist at the national lab today," she said to Dan, as he placed two dishes containing steak and cauliflower rice risotto on the bamboo placemats. She took a bite. "Mmm, cell-culture meat's getting gamier."

"Yep, I didn't over-grill it this time," he said. "What did the climatologist say?"

"The good news is he's eager to work with us. The not-so-good news is it'll take at least a month to do the analysis."

"Gee, that's a long time to keep this a secret." Dan paused with a forkful of steak in front of his mouth and raised an eyebrow. "You know about the theory of leaked secrets, right?"

"I vaguely remember you mentioning it."

"It's an anthropological pop culture axiom. In a community that doesn't follow top-secret protocols, the amount of time a secret can be kept confidential is inversely proportional to the newsworthiness of the secret. The Berkeley campus doesn't maintain top-secret clearance and the Proxima flyby is big news. I doubt you can keep this quiet for a month, or even a week."

Lita pursed her lips and held her chin. "If we announce soon, we risk causing anguish based on uncertainty. If we wait, we risk losing control of the details and context, at least initially."

"That could cause anguish too," Dan said.

"You're right. I need to talk to experts at the university and NASA. They'll help us do the public announcement right."

Lita d-messaged several UC Berkeley people to schedule an urgent meeting for tomorrow. She needed to head off any potential missteps. Her team's reputation and her tenure promotion were on the line. Despite the significance of the discovery, mishandling its announcement could taint her image in the eyes of her senior colleagues—at least among some prestigious but judgmental academic cliques.

14

Ambiguity

next day
day 4

* * *

Lita, her astronomy department's chairperson, and Berkeley's vice chancellor for communications sat around a plain wooden table in a drab, paneled conference room. At the head of the table, the wall screen projected a video of Dr. Lebron King, the director of the Planetary Defense Coordination Office, the NASA department funding Lita's ECN research.

"Are you sure about this?" Lebron said, interrupting Lita partway through her story of how ECN revealed the flyby. Lebron put his hands behind his head and leaned back in his chair in his office in Huntsville, Alabama. "Lita, you're more of a computer scientist than an astronomer. My PhD is in astronomy. I studied stars. Proxima is one of the stars in the three-star Centauri system. It's moving toward our solar system with a radial velocity of approximately twenty kilometers per second.

In about twenty-five thousand years it'll be closest to our sun at about three light-years away."

Lebron's patronizing mini lecture only slightly annoyed Lita because the sixty-four-year-old had been her longtime mentor, going back to her graduate school days at Michigan, where he'd been a professor. He was gruff but fatherly to her and other former students he'd taken a liking to.

"My team's also aware of the conventional facts about Proxima. That's why we were blown away when ECN revealed Proxima will experience a gravitational slingshot with its star couple, Alpha Centauri A and B. That slingshot will accelerate Proxima to about twelve thousand kilometers per second in a direction that's pointed 9.7 degrees more toward our solar system resulting in a 103-AU flyby in about 104 years."

"That's a bit less than five percent of the speed of light," Lebron said, shaking his head. "Stellar gravitational slingshot gives new meaning to the expression 'the stars are aligned.'"

The astronomy department chairperson chuckled and said, "I want to remind everyone that Proxima has a Goldilocks planet. Proxima b is in that solar system's habitable zone, with attributes possibly conducive to supporting life."

"Right," Lebron said. "Though that planet's surface habitability is uncertain given Proxima's extreme stellar wind and flares. Still, with a century of space travel tech development ahead of us, this flyby could give us our first and maybe sole opportunity to explore a Goldilocks planet."

Lita leaned back in her chair and crossed her legs. "The slingshot might perturb Proxima b's orbit in ways that affect its habitability. That'll be phenomenal to observe over the century."

After Lita briefed the three on Lain's biosphere analysis and

Luke's telescope research, they debated alternative announcement plans.

"The public has a hard time with ambiguity," Lebron said. "It'd be ideal to wait for some kind of flyby confirmation from Luke and the biosphere findings from Lain. If we announce too soon then have to modify what we said, we'll lose credibility with the public."

"I don't think we should postpone this for more than a week," Lita said.

"I agree with Lita," the vice chancellor said. "Waiting means we risk losing control of how this gets out. In any scenario, we should confidentially brief officials at the White House and Consortium."

Lita struggled between relying on the expertise in the meeting and her intuition. She wanted to be in control and decisive. "I don't want to flub this," she said. "We can't wait more than a week. We'll re-run the ECN analysis and brief government officials." The other three nodded their agreement. She added, "That'll take about five days. If everything goes as planned."

15

Collision

next day
day 5

* * *

Ryno rolled off Pari and lay spread-eagled on their bed. One of his favorite times for sex was the early morning while they were still dreamy. He wanted to doze off and have more sex with Pari later that morning, but Ricky Martin's "The Cup of Life" playing on his earbuds reminded him he needed to get ready for his intramural soccer game. He uncrumpled the bedsheet, pulled it over Pari's hips, and stretched in front of the window. Fog blanketed the flatlands of West Berkeley. He gathered his soccer helmet, pads, and cleats, then secured his impact-resistant sport monocle around both ears. A headline in his media feed caught his attention.

UC Berkeley professor discovers imminent asteroid collision with Earth.

Dumbfounded, Ryno fell back on the bed, ran his hand through his hair, and nudged Pari awake. "Pari, the world thinks we discovered an Earth collision. This obviously isn't the announcement plan—someone screwed up."

Pari turned over on her back. "You're trying to keep this secret?"

"Right, I must have forgotten to tell you."

"Well-uh, I told my dad. I tried again to convince him you're accomplished. So he'll approve of our relationship."

"You told your father?" Ryno stood and put his hands on top of his head. Her father was a former investment banker who'd been caught insider trading and jailed for a year. He had a pattern of trading secrets for money. "I think we know who leaked the discovery. Who else could it be?"

Pari sat up on her elbows. "You know I hate that. Treating my father like a criminal. He made a mistake decades ago. He's a changed man. If he told someone, why would he lie about it being a collision? That doesn't make sense." Pari turned on her side away from Ryno. "You've got to give him a second chance. If you want to win him over." She pulled the blanket over her shoulders. "And me."

"Okay, sorry. You're right. Why would he lie? Let's talk about this later. I need to send an urgent d-message to Lita."

Ryno dictated into his monocle.

= *Flyby leaked. But they got facts wrong. Checkout this media post.*

He didn't mention to Lita that he'd told Pari about the flyby and she'd told her father. Maybe he could at least keep that a secret.

16

Rock Climbing

seconds later

* * *

To stabilize her position on the rock-climbing simulator, Lita reached for a crack in the granite face. Her gecko glove's adhesion secured her grip. Ten feet above her, Dan had paused on a sliver of a ledge on the sheer wall to catch his breath. Immersed in a simulated free climb up Yosemite's El Capitan rock formation along The Nose route, Lita's focus on the challenge gave her a break from the all-consuming tension of the flyby. She'd rather be at the lab addressing that tension. But Dan had insisted on their weekly rock-climbing routine, to clear his mind. She needed to clear her mind too.

Despite her concentration, she couldn't ignore her monocle's emergency buzz. Something required her attention now. Maybe ECN had made another discovery.

After pausing her ascent to comprehend the significance of Ryno's d-message, she yelled, "Wall, end simulation." The virtual rock-climbing simulator's Yosemite vista vanished, revealing the room's domed ceiling and cylindrical green wall. Lita leaped off the simulated rock face from a height of about five feet and shouted, "Danno, the news is out. But they got the facts horribly wrong. They think it's a collision."

"What, a leak so soon?" Dan said, as his wiry frame spidered down the wall, using all the gecko patches on his cardinal red, skintight climbing suit. "We're definitely living in the Acceleration Age."

Lita removed her gloves and grabbed her screen out of her backpack. She unzipped the front of her blue-and-gold-striped climbing suit and paced along the base of the simulator while d-messaging with Berkeley's vice chancellor for communications.

During the ensuing discussion, Lita argued that her lab needed more time to verify the discovery before making a credible announcement. The vice chancellor agreed that the university wouldn't announce the actual flyby discovery but a brief official statement refuting the discovery of a collision was sensible.

Lita sat beside Dan at the climbing wall's edge. "Danno, why would someone leak the discovery and change the facts?"

"It could be random apocalyptic clickbait," Dan said, "that happens to be similar to the real discovery."

"That's too much of a coincidence. Could somebody be trying to undermine my research?"

Her monocle buzzed again with another emergency d-message. She read the message and flattened her lips.

Dan raised his eyebrow. "What now?"

She tilted her head back against the wall and sighed. "They're insisting that we announce the flyby at midday."

"Who's insisting?"

"Homeland Security."

"Why are they involved?"

"Apparently, the false announcement linked to cherry-picked excerpts from our ECN seminar. So the announcement looks official. It's causing public panic in some parts of the metaverse." She stood and closed her backpack. "Homeland Security wants me to clear the air. That means I need to explain what we really discovered. Otherwise, nobody will know who or what to believe." She sighed again. "Can't believe this is happening."

Dan put his arm around her shoulders. "I'm not surprised. Here's another anthropological pop culture axiom: The truth is hard to know. Facts can be complicated and change over time. But falsehoods can be absurd. Sometimes the more absurd the better, especially if the messengers are devious. Modern history's full of popular absurd falsehoods. Sandy Hook, Pizzagate, 9/11, QAnon, the Demon Parasite, even the Apollo moon landing."

"You're right. I need to deal with it head on."

Before departing the climbing center, Lita d-messaged an update to her lab team. Keeping them tightly in the loop was part of her strategy to maintain cohesion among the team's idiosyncratic personalities, especially because the botched announcement and need for an urgent remedy might upset Jase and anger Marc.

17

Rock Stars

noon the same day
day 5

* * *

"We didn't discover a collision. We discovered a solar-system flyby. And it'll peak in about a century," Lita said early in the press conference held in Smoot-Perlmutter Hall's virtual observatory. Floor-to-ceiling photorealistic images of deep-space phenomena taken by the Webb telescope lined the walls of the geodesic dome-shaped room the size of a basketball court. Most of the audience for this hastily assembled meeting were attending online. After her brief overview of the discovery, Lita projected a visualization of the flyby on the ceiling, noted when the stellar gravitational slingshot would occur, and pointed out the Goldilocks planet, Proxima b.

The Q and A session started with dozens of hands raised in person and online. A Toronto Times journalist transmitted his credentials to Lita's monocle. She blinked twice, giving him the floor. He stood. "Will we try to send a crewed mission to the Goldilocks planet?"

Lita turned to Lebron, attending from his Huntsville office via holographic link.

"NASA hasn't established any plans for this flyby yet," Lebron said. "I want to emphasize that the flyby's minimum orbit intersection distance is one hundred four years away. Nonetheless, this extraordinary discovery has already captured the imagination of our space agency planners. I'm sure we'll take advantage of the flyby opportunity."

"I have a question," a man shouted with a raspy voice from the back of the room. He had a bushy salt-and-pepper beard and a shaved head. His charcoal greatcoat hung unbuttoned on his broad shoulders, and his hair-thin wireframe monocle was almost imperceptible. "I'm Dr. Robert Bob, with the zine *Revelation News*. You abruptly scheduled this press conference after the supposedly false leak. When were you planning to announce this alleged discovery? And why were you keeping it secret?"

Lita glanced at Dan on the right side of the room and at the vice chancellor for communications on the other side. Her reply shouldn't sound evasive or defensive. But it also shouldn't fan hysterical speculation about calamitous flyby impacts. Her pause to consider the best response felt like forever, as all eyes in the room and on the internet-S were on her. "We had planned to do a series of pre-announcements to government officials and re-run ECN's analysis."

"Why?" Robert asked, running his hand over his beard. "Is there a reason to doubt the computer?"

Lita furrowed her brow. "No. But, given the discovery's immensity, we wanted to replicate our analysis." Maybe her answer had been too forthright. One question and a follow-up question were enough for this skeptic. She cut him off by pointing to a woman in the front of the room with her hand raised.

"Will the flyby impact our solar system and Earth?"

"Good question," Lita said. This aspect of the flyby needed to be mentioned. But it had to be conveyed matter-of-factly, not apprehensively. "Yes, but only in a minor way. Depending on where Proxima is relative to the alignments of Earth, our sun, and large planets like Jupiter, our planet's elliptical orbital distance from the sun will slightly increase by one to three million kilometers. That's about 1.34 percent. Scientists are currently assessing the impact, if any, on our biosphere."

After a few more straightforward questions, the press conference ended with a standing ovation.

As Lita walked off the podium, Ryno bounded over to her and turned his display to show her the Civil World's online citizen-verified poll. "You have an eighty-one percent approval rating," he said. "That's rock-star status."

Lita guffawed in reaction to Ryno's rock star comment and from her curiosity. Why did nineteen percent of the respondents not approve of her and the discovery? They couldn't disapprove of facts. Maybe they thought she was arrogant or elitist? Whatever, now wasn't the time to dwell on those naysayers. It was time to celebrate and then delve into the flyby's astrophysics. She made a big circular motion with her hand. "This is a pinnacle moment for our entire team. I'm so proud of us. We're all rock stars."

II

Part Two

18

Mentor

Trust dies but mistrust blossoms.
—*Sophocles*

* * *

next day
day 6
2033 January 19

* * *

Marc sat at an outdoor table at UC Berkeley's Free Speech Café and watched a group of students toss a Frisbee on the spacious sloping lawn across from the café. The smell of damp, freshly cut grass mixed with the cool air reminded him of his childhood home's backyard in Salt Lake City. Lita arrived with her slow-brewed coffee and sat across from Marc.

Marc pulled his monocle off his clean-shaven head and turned to Lita. "When we scheduled this breakfast last week, the possibility of discovering something like the Proxima flyby was inconceivable."

Lita poured half-and-half into her coffee. Her engagement ring glowed blue and green. "It's amazing. And it changes the whole reason for our meeting. Searching for collisions might not have been an impressive postdoc experience for your CV. But co-discovering this flyby, that's bound to attract lots of faculty positions."

"I appreciate your optimism," Marc said, rolling up the sleeves of his white, starched, Oxford shirt buttoned-up to his neck. "But ironically, our discovery has sidetracked my fixation on faculty jobs. I can't stop thinking about our flyby research. Maybe I should extend my postdoc another year?"

"I know what you mean. I can't focus on other things either—including my upcoming tenure review and wedding plans." Lita took a sip of her coffee. "You're welcome to stay another year. But it's time for you to launch your career. Our discovery will catapult your prominence. I'm here to help you get your dream position. That includes mentoring you to stay focused on the goal."

* * *

After their breakfast, Marc walked alongside Lita to the ECN lab. He had known that she had a fast gait. Next time he'd remember to bring his cane.

On the way, Lita's career advice calmed Marc's anxieties about providing for his wife and soon their newborn. He relished working with Lita, searching for Earth collisions, protecting the planet, doing good. He hadn't had the same sense of mission since leaving the Marine Corps. Earth collision research wasn't at the leading edge of astrophysics. Astrophysicists at the leading edge mostly did arcane research with no practical value. None of that mattered as much as working for a caring advisor. He'd take a bullet for Lita. As he'd done for his platoon's second lieutenant.

They turned the corner and entered the lush terrace of Smoot-Perlmutter Hall, the planet's newest temple to astrophysics.

"Stop right there," someone shouted. Lita froze in front of him and turned to her left. Five people dressed in black and carrying clubs rushed out from a creek bed that ran along the terrace. They wore black helmets with visors masking their faces. Marc looked for something to defend against them, a rock, tree branch, patio chair. Four of them surrounded him. One shoved the tip of his club against Marc's chest.

The fifth assailant grabbed Lita from behind, pressed his club under her chin, and wrenched her arm behind her back. "Let us in your lab," he said. "Give us the data."

"Data?" Lita said.

"The flyby secrets."

"What?" Lita winced. "Nothing's secret."

Beyond her, on the other side of the terrace, a bright blue light began flashing. A bystander must have set off the police emergency kiosk.

"You're lying," the assailant said and yanked Lita's arm farther back. "Just like you tried keeping the flyby a secret."

What was taking the police so long? Marc couldn't let his mentor suffer any longer. Using his Marine hand-to-hand combat skills, he lunged at the thug between him and Lita, knocking the guy off balance and reaching for his club. Just as Marc wrenched control of the club, a sharp pain on the side of his right knee stunned him. Falling to the ground, he swung at the ankle of the thug holding Lita. The guy shrieked in agony. Marc turned to swing at another thug. But a pounding on Marc's fist broke his grip. The club bounced on the ground.

Anticipating another blow, Marc rolled to his side and stretched for the club.

"University of California police! Drop your weapons." The voice from across the terrace froze the thugs. An officer ran toward the terrace. "Get on your knees. Raise your hands."

Despite being outnumbered five to one, the officer most likely wouldn't draw his weapon. That would breach UC police policy. Marc braced for a confrontation.

The thugs didn't engage the lone officer. Instead, they shoved Lita to the ground, threw an incendiary device at the building—distracting the officer—and ran back down the creek bed.

The scene became chaotic. After a few slow blinks, Marc's eyes closed. Sounds blurred together. The whine of an arriving ambulance grew louder. Somebody helped him onto a gurney. "Are you in pain?" a person asked him. He nodded, opened his eyes, and squinted from the sun shining behind an EMT's head, hovering over him.

The jab of a needle stung his arm. "This will blunt the pain," the EMT said.

"Is Lita okay?" Marc asked.

* * *

Marc woke up groggy. He tried to scratch the stubble on his face with his right hand, but the intravenous line limited his range of motion.

A nurse adjusted an ice bag around the welt on his hand. "How you feeling?"

"I've been better."

"X-rays show your hand only has a severe bruise. But your lateral collateral ligament on your right knee is torn from the trauma. We're fitting you with an exoskeleton crutch." She smiled. "You'll be up and walking in an hour."

"What happened to Professor Bloom? Is she in the hospital too?"

"The doctors already discharged her. She's shaken and bruised, but nothing serious."

"I need to call my wife."

"The professor gave us your wife's contact information. She's on her way."

* * *

Resting in his hospital room, Marc watched a news report of the Berkeley incident. He could cope with his hand and knee pain, just as he had coped with the combat injury that had shattered his pelvis. But he couldn't stop brooding about those thugs victimizing him and Lita.

During his Marine stint in the western Africa area of the A-civ World, he had battled miscreants who brutalized women and children. Sadly, he couldn't bring all of them to justice. By the time the US and the rest of the Civ World had abandoned the A-civ World, he'd developed a hatred for those who threatened the rule of law and civil society.

He wanted justice for himself and Lita. Revenge too.

19

Protest

next day
day 7

* * *

"Release the data, tell the truth. Release the data, tell the truth," the protesters chanted outside Lita's fifth-floor office window. Still shaken from the attack, Lita held Dan's arm as she limped along the bamboo floor to the open window overlooking the terrace of Smoot-Perlmutter Hall. Benna, her best friend, followed. On the stone terrace below, many of the dozens of protesters wore the same black-clad outfits and helmets her assailants had worn yesterday. Some carried signs with the phrases "Public University = Public Data" and "Academics R Kabalist-ics."

Jase tapped on Lita's open office door and joined the three at the window. "I grabbed one of their leaflets," he said.

Dan cautioned with his hands for Jase to take it slowly.

"Lita, would you like me to read it?" Jase asked.

She nodded and half-smiled.

"It says the protesters are members of an organization called The End of Earth Society. Their leader is Dr. Robert Bob."

"He's the guy at the press conference," Dan said, "who asked why you delayed the announcement and why the public should trust the ECN computer's AI."

Jase looked at the leaflet. "Indeed. Ap-apparently he's also the editor-in-chief of *Revelation News*."

"Now I get the connection," Lita said. She shuffled to a chair and eased into it. Jase's cogg nuzzled her leg. "Revelation, as in the Book of Revelation—the last book in the New Testament. It's apocalyptic."

Jase continued reading. "His organization believes that as Proxima nears, its gravity will act like a chain reaction on our solar system's outer planets and pull Earth away from the sun. That'll turn Earth into a frozen desert like Mars. Only cabals of academics who know about this cataclysm are preparing for it. And only they will survive in secret underground cities under construction."

"Metaverse conspiracists," Benna said.

Jase turned the leaflet over. "They claim the university's initial reluctance to announce the flyby proves that the academics aren't forthright."

"They're an apocalyptic cult," Dan said.

"The tone of Bob's questions spooked me," Benna said. "I web-searched him after the press conference. He has a PhD in integrative biology. Up until a few years ago, he'd worked as a science journalist. He was fired and blacklisted, he claims, because he uncovered evidence that huge swaths of what Bob calls 'the industrial news complex' are controlled by secret groups who foment controversy to drive the twenty-four-hour news cycle."

"I don't know about that," Dan said. "But if my parents had named me Bob Bob, I'd think the world was conspiring against me too."

Benna chuckled.

"What's with all those shiny black helmets?" Jase asked.

"My monocle flashed a snippet about them," Dan said. "The shiny material is Mylar. It shields their brains from electromagnetic radiation. They think the government uses electromagnetic field transmissions to influence their feelings like joy, anger, and empathy."

"I'd like one of those helmets," Jase said.

"It's paranoia," Lita said.

"Technically, it's plausible. I wouldn't put it past the US government or some other spy a-agency to do something like that."

"Jase, why're you so distrustful of the government?" Benna asked.

"This isn't something I like to talk about," Jase said. He kneeled to pet his cogg. "My father dedicated his career to the CIA. He worked as an en-encryption expert. He died last year in Korea—his home country. Nobody in the government will give my mom and me a straight answer about his death." Jase closed his eyes and sniffled. His voice quivered. "They say it was suicide. And the details are a matter of national security." He shook his head and took a deep breath, composing himself. "No, I think they're covering up a CIA mistake. An operation gone wrong."

Jase's cogg placed its paw on Jase's foot and stroked it.

"I understand the hole that can leave," Lita said. Her eyes moistened as she reached to hug Jase. "My parents died scouting archaeological sites in Namibia." She wiped a tear from her cheek. "Their bodies were never recovered. I'm not sure of the details. The uncertainty's hollowing." She sniffed. "We have to move on. That's what they would've wanted."

A knock on the office door interrupted Lita's embrace. "Sorry to barge in," a university police officer said. "We're getting intelligence that the protesters plan to ransack your lab. We're evacuating and barricading the building. I need to escort you out the north side emergency exit."

Lita held Dan's arm as they departed the building, surrounded by police officers. While driving home with a police escort, she d-messaged Marc in the hospital and Ryno in class to inform them of the spiraling situation. Keeping the team connected was more critical than ever. Damage to the ECN lab would demoralize them. She wanted to harden them for the devastating setback to their research. She also needed to steel herself. The attack on her and the lab made her just want to go to her office, lock the door, and bury herself in her research.

20

Goad

an hour later

* * *

Bob stood in the middle of the protest and egged on his followers. Out of the corner of his eye, he watched the university police department's RV-size mobile command vehicle pull into Smoot-Perlmutter Hall's parking lot, accompanied by police on electric bikes and buzzing drones. It looked like an aircraft carrier with its armada of support craft.

His spy inside the police command vehicle sent an encrypted text message to Bob's visor.

= *Careful what you say. Drone above eavesdropping on your conversation, even whispers.*

Bob's lips turned up. Time to goad the cops. He gestured for the three lieutenants among his minions to gather around him. "At sundown, we'll storm the building and take over the quantum computer lab. If we can't get the data, we'll smash the computer so nobody can use it."

Another text appeared on his visor.

= *Police chief concerned about number of protesters. More coming from BART train station. He's calling for reinforcements.*

Two police officers walked onto the fourth-floor balcony of Smoot-Perlmutter Hall. One officer held up a mobile microphone. "Attention. Attention. Your assembly is declared unlawful. Immediately disperse, or we'll take action to clear the area."

Bob turned to the crowd around him. "See how violently they cling to their power. They fear us. Fear we'll expose their lies to the world."

He lifted his megaphone. "Attention. Attention. We the people declare the public university's secret research unlawful. Immediately release all the data, or we'll take action to obtain it."

The protesters cheered Bob and jeered the police. Bob ran his hand through his beard as more of his protesters piled onto the terrace.

More text streamed across his visor. He smirked. His spy had plugged him into the police chief's d-messages requesting backup.

= *Hello mayor. My campus police r getting overwhelmed by protesters at sp hall. I'm worried about damage to billion $ computer. Can city's police help with reinforcements?*

= *Greetings chief. News stories indicate that univ could be holding back flyby data like it held back flyby discovery. Protesters might have a valid grievance. I'd be run out of office if we support ur police, especially if you use force. Sorry I can't help.*

Bob's visor went blank. Damn, was his spy caught? After a long moment a new text flashed:

= *Chief authorizing use of proprioceptor inhibitor spray.*

Bob shook his head and mumbled, "This chief's a novice."

He pulled a pain-deadening inhaler out of his pocket and gestured to his lieutenants to do the same. The inhaler wouldn't prevent the spray from immobilizing them, but it would blunt the pain.

Dozens of police entered the terrace, wearing face masks and wielding weapons that looked like industrial-grade water guns. Three officers encircled Bob. He gave them an evil smile. "This has been a peaceful protest," he yelled and smoothed out his beard again. "The corrupt university leaders will regret using chemical weapons to stop our free speech."

Officers sprayed Bob and several other protesters, bringing them to the ground.

"This is an assault on our free speech rights," Bob screamed while flailing on his back. "Mark my words. The whole university will regret this."

He half lifted his arm and pointed at the officer who sprayed him. "You call yourself a peace officer? I'll make sure you're the first to get fired and jailed."

The officers cuffed Bob, waited a moment for the proprioceptor inhibitor to wear off, and led him to the police van. Before they removed Bob's helmet, his spy sent one more text.

= Protesters dispersing. Police see social media messages planning protests tomorrow. Police also aware of protesters doxxing the home addresses of the ECN lab members. Chief worried about getting stretched thin to protect ECN lab and team. Next phase of your plan should work too.

* * *

Bob and his three lieutenants trudged into the police station's holding room. Police officers secured his handcuffs to the metal armrests of seats along the room's concrete wall. The chief and his officers walked into the adjacent lobby and slammed the glass door behind them. It bounced and remained ajar.

Bob was surprised—no, amazed. He could not only see the chief, he could also just barely make out his conversation. He put his finger to his lips, motioning to his lieutenants to quiet their griping.

Apparently, the university's vice chancellor for administration had been sitting in that room, waiting for the chief.

"I'm pleased to report we saved the quantum computer from vandals," the chief said to the vice chancellor.

Bob sneered. He was a truth fighter, not a vandal.

"Chief, I appreciate the situation was tense and you wanted to make quick decisions," the vice chancellor said. "But you need to keep in closer contact with our crisis response team. You're new here and there's a lot to learn."

"I didn't authorize the use of weapons," the chief said, "until we had a tangible threat to a major loss of property, the billion-dollar computer."

"The quantum computer wasn't in danger," the vice chancellor said. She frowned and flipped up her herringbone-style monocle. "For cybersecurity reasons, we try not to make this well known. SP Hall only has a relatively inexpensive human interface to the quantum computer. The actual computer complex is in a secure location, miles off the west coast. There, it's spread across a set of interconnected sunken barges sitting on the seafloor two hundred feet below the ocean surface. Submerging it in the Pacific current's forty-degree water makes it easier to keep the computer at near absolute zero."

Bob's eyes widened. He hadn't known that. It'd be quite a coup to learn the computer's whereabouts.

The chief glanced at his handset. "Now I know why Professor Bloom had sent a d-message thanking me for saving the building but didn't mention saving the computer."

The vice chancellor flipped down her monocle. "So, Chief, using proprioception weapons to quell the protest will be criticized as a disproportionate response. An overreaction to the threat. That'll likely result in an investigation that embarrasses the university leadership. To lessen this backlash, you need to release the protesters."

Bob gave a thumbs-up to his three lieutenants.

The chief bowed his head. "Okay. I take full responsibility. Next time, I'll confer with the crisis team." He flipped down his monocle and turned to his officers. "Let's release Bob."

The chief walked toward the holding room and muttered, "We'll see who overreacted if Bob and his mob harass the lab team at their homes."

"Chief, I didn't hear you clearly," the vice chancellor said.

"I said we'll update Professor Bloom and her ECN team after releasing Bob."

The chief uncuffed Bob. Bob leaned his face forward, locked eyes with the chief, and mocked him with an exaggerated kissing gesture. Bob turned and sauntered out of the station, already planning the next phase of his strategy to achieve his life's mission. The reason why he was put on Earth.

His prior investigative journalism had revealed how cabals controlled key dynamics of the Civ World. Most people were too naive to comprehend how they were pawns in a great game, in part because they'd been bamboozled by the industrial media complex in cahoots with other cabals. Even if some of his conspiratorial assertions stretched the truth, they achieved his mission of sensitizing the public to the machinations of the global puppet masters. And he knew how to come right up to, but not cross the line of the DF-DS law. He was a master at inspiring mass cynicism. A genuine patriotic truth fighter.

21

Threats

next day
day 8

* * *

Lita took a sip of her French onion soup and leaned back in her seat against the mahogany wall of the Women's Faculty Club. Quiet conversations and clanking silverware echoed in the cavernous dining room. Photos of the campus from the previous centuries lined the walls and dignified the ambiance.

"How's my bestie feeling?" Benna asked, sitting across from Lita at the redwood table and holding a forkful of spicy cricket salad.

"Honestly, I'm still shaken," Lita said. "I never thought I'd be assaulted like that. But my team's doing okay. We're proud of our high poll rating. I can't wait to get back to the lab and learn more about the flyby, for example, how will it affect Proxima b."

"I feel your enthusiasm and your rating's impressive. But

do you know about the conspiracy theories swirling around the metaverse?"

"What conspiracies?"

"I'll show you." Benna unrolled her screen, entered a search for "flyby conspiracy memes," and turned her screen toward Lita. "Here are about a dozen memes. Most are just fantasies of blithering DOTEs. But some have traction."

"DOTEs?" Lita said.

"Lita, my friend, you gotta get your head out of your lab more. You're oblivious to the flyby conspiracies and you don't know what DOTE means? It's the new pop culture acronym for Distrusters of Technology Elites. It's like a cross between a dope and a Luddite."

"Pop culture doesn't interest me. It's a distraction." Lita touched the screen. "Okay, let's see this meme with the highest rating, fifteen percent 'Berkeley academics fabricate flyby to blaspheme the Bible, creationism, and Earth's true history.'" She pursed her lips and narrowed her eyes. "What? That's absurd. I don't get the connection."

"I read about that yesterday," Benna said. "The logic's spurious, but the messenger's beguilingly charismatic. She's a religious fundamentalist crusader named Lourdes Graham. She alleges your social media accounts were hacked and revealed you're active on several atheist forums. And you're also a member of the Union for the Mitigation of Societal Stratification. Lourdes accuses the union of trying to limit the God-given rights of Americans to live where they want and with whom they want to live among."

"All lies, except for the union. I'm glad you introduced me to it. We know it's not trying to limit freedom to—"

Lita turned to her side. A commotion at the entrance to

the restaurant interrupted her response. Despite objections from the Faculty Club staff, a man and woman, who looked like students, wanted to enter the dining room. While the man argued with the maître d', the woman scanned the tables. When she locked eyes with Lita, she strode toward her. The man followed.

Benna stood and moved in front of Lita. "What's this about?" She extended her arm toward the woman. "Don't come any closer."

Lita moved her hands over her knife and fork.

Conversations in the restaurants ceased.

The woman raised her hands. "Hello, Professor Bloom. We're student journalists with *The Daily Californian*. Sorry to disturb your lunch and make such a scene." The journalist looked around the room. "Can we interview you about the flyby and yesterday's protest?"

Lita glanced at Benna. She shrugged.

"Sure, I have nothing to hide," Lita said and took another sip of her soup.

"Okay, we're recording," the man said, pointing his camcorder at Lita.

"Let's start with the discovery," the woman said. "Why keep it secret?"

Lita flattened her lips and glanced at Benna again. Why did the journalist start with an accusation?

"We weren't hiding it from the public. We wanted to make sure we got everything right first. That's what scientists do."

Instead of letting the woman make another accusation, Lita continued. "Our lab isn't holding back information. In fact, in the spirit of openness, we're distributing ECN results on the internet-S, in real-time. Dozens of other research centers are investigating the flyby. For example, this morning, Professor Luke Johnson at the University of Texas informed me of an upgraded space telescope his lab team is now aiming at Proxima. The initial data had some interesting patterns that might indicate the start of a gravitational slingshot."

"Let's remember to follow up with the UT professor," the woman said to her cameraman then turned back to Lita. "What about the rumors that you're anti-religion? They say you concocted the flyby to discredit religious canon."

Lita grimaced. "What religious canon? I don't get it. The flyby isn't a concoction." She sighed. "I'll admit I've questioned fundamentalist religion in the context of science. I want to emphasize that I respect other people's beliefs. Also I value the role that faith can have in times of crisis—when people risk losing hope. Faith can inspire people to do wonderful things. As a matter of fact, my fiancé is a person of faith."

Lita didn't elaborate that Dan's faith was westernized Buddhism, not a conventional theist religion.

"Okay, cut," the cameraman said. "It's streaming now, across the internet-S and the metaverse. Thanks for your time, professor."

"That seemed to go smoothly," Benna said, when the students were out of earshot.

Lita didn't respond. She looked down at the floor and focused on her monocle.

"Something wrong?" Benna asked.

"I'm getting a stream of death threats." Her heart started pounding. "I should have told them to restrict the distribution to only the internet-S. Also I shouldn't have been so forthright."

Benna reached for Lita's hand. "You did the right thing. Those trolls have no right or reason to harass you."

Lita's field of vision narrowed. "I'm getting nauseous. Help me to the restroom."

22

Raid

next morning
day 9

* * *

Lita admired her kitchen window's view of the fog blanketing the city, then sat at the kitchen table, propped up her screen, and played a recently posted video. Dan positioned himself over her shoulder and caressed her arm. The video showed Lita seated at a conference panel table saying, "Fundamentalist religion is a conspiracy theory. It professes that subjugation to a priesthood and obedience to a dogma is required to get into a fairyland place called heaven and avoid a make-believe place called hell—for eternity."

"I never said that. It's a deep fake," she said, scooping up a spoonful of her crunchy mealworm cereal.

Dan pointed at the screen. "Damn, three million views."

She propped her head on her palm. "It's based on a real video of me speaking at a conference last year. But those weren't my words."

He sat beside her and showed the negative test result of his morning blood-prick for disease markers. She showed him her negative test too.

Lita scrolled down her screen. "Check out this story. It's about the fundamentalist crusader Lourdes Graham and hardline US Congressman Charles Foster. The two are pressing for an investigation by Homeland Security's recently established Free Speech Force. 'Foster and Graham want the FSF to determine whether Berkeley Professor Amelita Bloom is guilty of DF-DS, Distributing Fabrications to Disrupt Society.'" Lita looked up at Dan. "DF-DS? I thought that only applied to politics, not science."

"An excerpt of the law's definition is coming up on my monocle. Here it is. 'All expressions, whether oral, written or otherwise, containing falsehoods that actually or are intended to be detrimental to the health, well-being, or stability of the nation or its citizens are punishable to the full extent of the law.'"

She rubbed her face. "Danno, my stomach's in knots." Her voice quivered. "First the death threats and now this DF-DS accusation. Why can't I do my research in peace?"

He brushed her hair to the side. "We'll get through this together. We know the truth. This'll blow over soon." He stood and stepped to the window. "Let's get ready to go to work."

* * *

While Lita was changing into her work clothes, a pounding at the condo's front door startled her.

A person at the door shouted, "Professor Amelita Bloom, this is the United States Homeland Security's Free Speech Force. We have a warrant to search, probe, and, if necessary, seize your property. This is part of an official investigation into allegedly distributing fabrications to disrupt society. Open the door, or we'll forcibly enter."

Lita followed Dan to the door. He looked through the peephole. She received flashes on her monocle. "Danno, I'm getting d-messages from Marc and Ryno. FSF officers raided their homes. And Jase says they're at the lab."

Dan opened the door.

"I'm FSF Officer Jeremiah O'Brien. The court order should now be accessible via your monocles. My two field technicians are here to capture snapshots of the data on your digital devices. Under penalty of law, the court order obligates you to disclose to us all your devices with at least one gigabyte of digital storage."

Lita walked hand in hand with Dan through their home, identifying their digital devices to the FSF technicians. She had nothing to hide. But this intrusion wasn't right. Should she identify all her digital devices? What about her e-photo album? It looked like an innocuous book alongside the row of textbooks on the bottom shelf of their wall of books. Surely these intruders didn't need to copy her childhood pictures. Should she take a stand just on principle?

Her father had told her a story that when he was sixteen, a police officer in Mexico pulled him over for supposedly speeding. The officer asked to see what was in the car's trunk. Her father thought it was empty. He opened it for the officer. It contained alcohol and cannabis. He hadn't known that his friends had stashed their party supplies in the trunk that morning. He ended up in a Mexico jail cell for the night.

After pointing out all her devices except the album, she sat with Dan on their couch and tried to hold back sniffles. "The people who are supposed to protect us are ransacking our home," she whispered to Dan.

"We have nothing to hide," Dan said, cringing. "Who knew religious evangelists could have such influence over a US government agency?"

While the two technicians performed their digital interrogation, the officer held his gaze on Lita, squinting his eye that wasn't hidden behind his silver-mirrored monocle. Lita turned away from the officer. His monocle might have been recording her minute reactions to the interrogation, searching for facial clues indicating her guilt.

The officer broke the silence. "What do you know about Jase Park-Muller's private life?"

Lita snickered. "Private life? Jase only has one life, his lab research."

"What about his interest in anarchy?"

"What?" Lita snickered again. "Lab research is his sole interest."

"That's his public persona. Maybe you don't know him as well as you think."

"Are you interrogating Lita?" Dan asked.

"We're done," one of the technicians said from across the room.

The officer nodded, placed three electronic nodes around the room, and clicked a few buttons on his mobile screen. "This," he said while peering at his screen, "will triangulate on signals from all digital devices in the vicinity, including any you didn't disclose."

Lita's heart thumped. "Damn it," she said under her breath.

The officer pointed his screen at the wall of books, bent down, grabbed the album, and opened it. "What's this?" he said, holding up the digital screen behind the cover.

Dan glared at Lita and raised an eyebrow.

"Sorry, I forgot about that," she said. "It's just old photos."

"This lack of compliance will be reported," the officer said and handed the album to one of the technicians.

"What if there's nothing problematic on the device?" Dan said, his eyes still fixed on Lita.

"Doesn't matter," the officer said. "This proves she didn't comply. It implies guilt."

The officer packed the three nodes. "We're done for now." At the door, he turned back to Lita. "It may please you to know we posted a small garrison of armed FSF officers at your lab's building to halt the protesting. We need to secure your lab for our investigation. We'll allow you and your team to work there. At least for now."

"You sure you can keep the protesters away?" Lita asked.

"Unlike your university police, we have no restraints on using lethal force."

"Are we safe here?" Lita asked.

"Safe?" The officer tilted his head. "Safeness is a story we tell ourselves."

The officer turned and slammed the door shut. Lita put her head in Dan's lap and sobbed.

He stroked her hair. "It'll be okay."

"I should've told them about the album."

"Can't blame you for your defiance," he said.

"Should we get away from here? Leave the city?"

Dan turned to the window. "This building has lots of security.

We'd be on our own in some isolated place."

She sat up and rubbed her face. "Could the FSF legally restrict us from accessing ECN? What's next, home confinement?"

"We should get a lawyer."

23

Anarchist

next day
day 10

* * *

A d-message flashed on Jase's desktop screen, interrupting his early morning work in the ECN lab.

= *Son, I know u don't bother with social media or news. So I'm sending you this link from today's news.*

Jase responded.

= *Mom, how r u?*

= *I'm ok. I'm worried about u & free speech force goons. Remember, ur cogg can comfort & also protect u. I gotta go.*

Jase sighed. Ever since his dad died, his mom had become reclusive. Never willing to talk much. She knew that Jase was a *NoSoMe*—a person who didn't bother with social media or use a monocle. So he wasn't distracted by metaverse noise and didn't have to worry about death threats—like those harassing Lita.

He stroked Cogg's back and considered whether to open the

news link. His mom rarely asked him to do anything. He should honor her request.

The link opened a video of Congressman Foster making a media announcement. "I've been informed by the director of the Free Speech Force that its DF-DS investigation is already producing results. Yesterday they learned that the Berkeley lab's graduate student, Jase Park-Muller, is an anarchist. Here's a video snippet of Park-Muller at a riot booing when a speaker mentioned the Consortium of the Civ World."

Jase paused the video. Yes, he had booed. He had tried not to stand out. The surveillance video technology's ability to zoom in on an individual in the large crowd was scary impressive.

He resumed playing the video. "The FSF now considers Park-Muller a suspect in a manipulation of the quantum computer to falsify a flyby to spread fear and panic. The FSF is preparing to indict Park-Muller on the criminal charge of creating and distributing fabrications intended to disrupt society. That has a minimum prison sentence of five years. The FSF is also considering indictments of the other Berkeley lab members on the lesser criminal charge of co-conspiring, redistributing, or otherwise knowingly facilitating the distribution of fabrications to disrupt society. That has a minimum prison term of two years."

The video ended with an image of Jase's UC Berkeley photo ID card below the caption *Anarchists are state enemies* and above the statement *This news reel proudly sponsored by the Congressional Patriots Caucus.*

Jase grimaced and turned to the lab's door, ajar as usual. Lab members were slack about security. He closed the door and engaged its biometric lock, hoping it still worked. He hadn't used it in months.

Cogg whimpered. Jase picked it up and hugged it. Years in prison. Not able to do his research. He'd go insane. His father's experience informed him that parts of the US government couldn't always be trusted. Innocence or guilt sometimes didn't matter. Politics and power mattered. Should he flee to Canada and ask for asylum? He could continue his ECN research remotely. He turned to the window and studied the empty quad. The FSF was probably surveilling him. Its officers would stop him at the border.

He pressed his forehead against Cogg's neck and closed his eyes. Who could he turn to for help? Maybe he did need friends. His mom had been right about that.

24

Dissension

next day
day 11

* * *

Lita sat at her desk in the ECN lab and doom-scrolled through web pages of flyby conspiracy memes. Over the past twenty-four hours, they'd been feeding on each other and metastasizing. Should she ignore them? A rhythmic clicking in the hallway interrupted her. The clicking grew into a clanking, like a mechanized evil meme was coming for her. She turned around and peered at the door.

Marc stormed into the room with the aid of his exoskeleton crutch. He glanced at Lita and confronted Jase. "You frickin' manipulated ECN reports."

Lita stepped in front of Marc and held up her hands to keep the situation from getting physical. Jase had always rubbed Marc the wrong way. Marc's patriotic, community-oriented mindset had no place for Jase's apolitical, unsocial attitude.

Marc turned to Lita. "How do we know he isn't manipulating ECN reports? He's always in the lab. He redirected ECN away from our collision research. He made the first flyby observation. And he opposes the Civil World's Consortium."

Jase reached over to put his hand firmly on his cogg. "My eighty-hour work weeks at the lab show my dedication to our research." He turned to his cogg and lowered his eyes. "We just happened upon that rally. It wasn't a riot. It came together for an im-important cause—global human welfare, not an-anarchy. I didn't go on the march. We walked back to the ECN lab in the same direction as the march. Cogg has the archived video to prove it."

"I'm not going to jail because of your warped beliefs," Marc said. "Let's check that robot's video. See if you booed when the Consortium was mentioned."

"I admit it. I booed. The Consortium's hiding documents that reveal the terrible conditions in the A-civ World." Jase looked up but kept his hand firmly on his cogg. "Ev-everyone around me was booing."

Jase's distress paused Marc's attack. Marc's apparent empathy surprised Lita.

Standing in the lab's doorway, Ryno had observed the argument and continued the accusations. "Jase, did you leak the discovery to the public?"

"Course not. Why would I do that? And claim it's a collision?"

"To attract attention," Ryno said.

Lita positioned herself between Jase and the others. "Guys, we need to stick together. We can't let our real enemies divide us. Those are the people who're actually distributing fabrications to disrupt society and our research."

Her monocle flashed an urgent voice call from her astrophysicist collaborator, Professor Luke Johnson at the University of Texas. At Lita's request, he'd been studying Proxima for conventional signs of an emerging gravitational slingshot.

But she was distracted from responding to Luke's call by two people who barged into the lab—without asking permission to enter. One wore a jacket with "FBI" on it in large yellow letters.

The taller of the two intruders was the FSF officer with the silver-mirrored monocle who had led the interrogation of Lita's home.

"ECN team, listen up. I'm FSF Officer Jeremiah O'Brien and this is FBI Agent Shelley Leight." He pointed to Lita and Jase. "More negative news has been posted about the professor and now the grad student. That's fueling growing doubt about the flyby. Your online ratings are below five percent, which the FBI refers to as 'lynch-mob levels of disapproval.'"

"Your low poll ratings are inciting vigilantism," Shelley said, "and the FBI is aware of groups plotting to attack the lab and you all. You're not safe, even in your homes." She flipped up her monocle. "My FBI office is offering you refuge. We recommend you each be placed under government protection at separate, secret locations until we get past this hysteria."

Jase stood. "Offering or demanding?" His hand no longer rested on his cogg. "I'm not afraid of those threats. Besides, why should we trust the government? And why do we need to be separated? Maybe the FSF is stoking this backlash to get us to turn on each other—to help the DF-DS in-investigation."

The cogg seemed to sense Jase's agitation. That triggered the robot to stand up its synthetic fur and puff itself to the size of a wolf. It opened its metallic mouth like a cobra, bared its silver canines, and growled as loud as a grizzly at the person Jase shouted at—the FSF officer.

Lita gasped. Months ago Jase had mentioned that his cogg had a bully-defense mode. But the comfort pet's transformation into a menacing-looking demon shocked Lita.

The barrel of a weapon instantly popped up from the officer's helmet and bore down on the cogg. The officer glared at Jase. "Tell your machine pet to stand down. Or I'll blast a nine-millimeter-wide laser through its freakin face."

Lita reached out to grab Jase's arm. The speed at which the officer had locked and loaded his weapon was scary impressive. He must have a neural interface to the laser. Would there be a robot-human battle in her lab? Just minutes ago, the cogg could've also attacked Marc or Ryno during their heated argument with Jase. That explained why Jase had kept his hand on the cogg. It also explained how his robot companion emboldened Jase, despite the physical threats against him. He had a superhuman bodyguard. It'd be nice to have one of those for herself.

After a long moment, Jase reached down to put his hand back on his cogg. It toggled back to calm mode.

Shelley raised her hands to her shoulders. "Separation is an enhanced security precaution. It improves your safety," she said, breaking the tension-filled stand-off between Jase and the FSF officer. "It's based on the success of the FBI's Witness Protection Program."

"Regardless of whether you accept the protection plan," the FSF officer said, "the FSF is banning you from posting on the internet-S, interacting with the public, collaborating with other researchers, and accessing the quantum computer until further notice. In a moment, the documents officiating your bans should be accessible on your monocles."

"We need a few minutes to discuss this," Lita said. "Can you step out of the lab?"

The FSF officer crossed his arms. "Whatever. Don't take too long."

The team huddled together. "Our safety is my highest priority," Lita said. "With all the death threats, I'm feeling vulnerable. We're not safe."

"If we're targets," Marc said, "our family and friends could be inadvertently hurt."

"Let's do the isolation," Lita said.

Ryno nodded and looked at Jase.

"That's all I have is my mom and Cogg," Jase said. "She's reclusive. Cogg can protect me and itself. That's assuming these threats are real, not fomented by harmless petty agitators and amplified by bots."

"Violence against democratically elected officials and other societal leaders is real," Marc said. "Why don't you think violence against leading-edge scientists can't be real?"

Jase looked away from Marc and didn't answer.

"Jase, please take this seriously," Lita said. "You're a key member of our team."

Jase sighed. "Fine. For a few days."

When the team re-engaged the two government officials, Ryno glared at the FSF officer and used his middle finger to flip down his monocle. That alarmed Lita, because Ryno's action was considered an insult, like flipping off a person with a middle finger. The FSF officer scowled at Ryno and Lita. This was now personal.

Together, the team exited the building. Four armed FBI squads awaited them. Jase carried his cogg. The officers put each lab member in the windowless cabin of separate military vehicles.

* * *

The FBI agents drove Lita to her home to pick up extra personal belongings and then to a secret location. While at her house, she was allowed to have a brief call with Dan to explain the situation. He agreed that accepting the FBI offer would be best for her safety.

Now powerless, Lita hunched over on the bench seat in the vehicle's cab. Her lab was under siege from apocalyptic conspiracy groups, religious extremists, and even the US government.

Losing the opportunity to follow up with Luke at UT Austin before the FSF ban also frustrated her. She and Luke were friendly, going back to when they were at the University of Michigan. They'd even dated briefly. Luke had a swagger underpinned by his astrophysics brilliance. Using his unmatched expertise in low-frequency astronomy, he'd practically reinvented the field of radio and microwave telescopes.

A few days ago, Luke had followed through on her request to aim his lab's recently enhanced space telescope at Proxima. They were getting some intriguing early data and he said he'd follow up with her when he learned more. If what Luke had learned was mundane why would he have called her? A call implied he had something special to tell her. But if he'd confirmed the flyby then why not immediately announce it and end this hell for her? Maybe he'd called to give her bad news. Apologize for shutting down his Proxima flyby work due to government pressure, or something like that.

* * *

While lying on his back in the FBI vehicle cabin's bench seat and daydreaming, it occurred to Jase that ECN continued to iterate and reveal Proxima's path further forward in time and backward too. How far could ECN go, and would it find anything else interesting? That piqued his curiosity and imagination. It also intensified his frustration. He needed to regain access to ECN.

25

Despondence

What loneliness is more lonely than distrust?
—*George Eliot*

* * *

next day
day 12

* * *

Lita's mobile screen on the safe house's kitchen table beeped twice. A d-message had arrived. Her first communication with the outside world since sequestering. It gave her a reason to get out of bed. She'd been trying to meditate, but was mostly daydreaming, or more accurately ruminating for who knows how long. The message had to be from a US government agency. The FSF firewall blocked all other communications to enforce its ban on the lab team. Maybe the FBI was informing her it was safe enough to leave this hellhole.

The air in the kitchen was musty, probably mold. The laminate dinette set was pushed against a wall. Above the table, a wall clock missing its hour hand ticked. Out the kitchen window, a tall wood fence with peeling white paint blocked views of anything and anyone. Decades ago, this must have been military base housing for some junior personnel.

She sat at the table in front of the screen. Wow, a d-message from Ryno.

= *Hello ECN team. I hacked fsf security & set up* this stealth comm channel. *Dan & my girlfriend, Pari, are on it too. Get on the channel & let's watch* this FSF news update *together.*

Lita clicked the links and adjusted the screen's volume. Commiserating on the group channel might rebuild her team's camaraderie.

"Next up," the newscaster said, "the FSF's investigation of the Berkeley team is encountering difficulties and could take longer than expected." The feed switched to a five-second commercial.

What now? More bad news? Maybe she should go back to bed.

The newscaster returned. "The reason for the delay, the FSF claims, is that the ECN technology is esoteric. Only specially skilled people understand how the neural net uses the quantum computer to produce results. The FSF can't easily determine whether someone fabricated the ECN's flyby report. Despite the investigatory challenges, the University of California has put Professor Bloom on academic probation pending the investigation's results. Some astrophysicists and computer scientists are questioning the fundamentals of Bloom's ECN technology."

Lita scratched her head. That couldn't be right. It was probably reverberations of unsubstantiated rumors in the metaverse.

After the news snippet ended, the team's comm channel fell

silent. Everyone was probably in shock—like her. Who wouldn't be angry about the DF-DS allegations, worried about the death threats, and now despondent about the news of a protracted FSF investigation?

A mere seven days ago, Lita had relished how she and her lab team were on top of the world. Now they'd hit rock bottom. Yesterday she'd assumed her tenure promotion was inevitable. Today she was on academic probation. Her parents would be so disappointed if they were alive. Would Dan still love her if she lost her academic career? She had no plan B.

Her team's cohesion had broken down too. Marc and Ryno didn't trust Jase. Jase didn't trust anyone, especially the government. Even Lita wondered whether they should trust ECN. Maybe its underlying machine learning on how objects move in space wasn't trained enough to use on three-star systems. Several colleagues in her field had mentioned the n-body problem in orbital mechanics and questioned the fundamentals of her research. Could this hellacious situation have stemmed from a computational inaccuracy? Her imposter syndrome spiraled. Exhausted, she lay flat on the linoleum floor with her hands folded over her forehead and her eyes closed.

Dan broke the silence. "Hey, team. My faith in humanity makes me confident. Eventually you'll be proven innocent."

Lita loved Dan's optimism. She needed to step up and show confidence too. That would help her team's morale and please Dan. She sat up. "Dan's right. We need to trust each other, trust our technology, and trust that other researchers will soon verify our discovery."

"But how?" Ryno said. "I thought Jase told us no other researchers have the technology to foresee a stellar gravitational slingshot."

Nobody responded. Lita flopped back down. Ryno was probably right.

Marc didn't take part in the discussion. He was likely brooding. His once budding academic career looked as dead as Lita's.

Minutes of silence passed, as if everyone had wandered off the group comm channel.

Lita ruminated on Ryno's comment about other researchers. She sat up. "Wait a second. Maybe not," she mumbled and walked to her screen.

= *Danno, you still on the channel?*
= *Uh huh.*
= *At the same time the fbi and fsf barged into my lab, prof luke johnson at ut austin tried to phone me. A few days ago I had asked him to focus his lab's recently upgraded space telescope at Proxima. Maybe he had an important update. Please contact him.*
= *Absolutely.*
= *I love you Danno*
= *Love you too. We'll get through this together.*

* * *

After the group discussion ended, Pari d-messaged an emoji of a sad cat face with hearts to Ryno via the channel he'd hacked.

Ryno teared up. This was the first night in over a month that he wasn't with Pari.

He walked out to the concrete stoop of the bunkhouse he was cloistered in. The night was dry, cool, and clear. The faint drone of cars on a highway mixed with cricket chirps. He set his handset to play The Who's "Love, Reign o'er Me" at concert hall volume and crooned along with the lyrics. During the song's crescendo another d-message arrived via his channel, this one from Jase.

= *Ryno, how'd u get past fsf online security?*
= *It's complicated. Why do u ask?*
= *I need to regain access to ecn.*

If he helped Jase would he get in more legal trouble, maybe a harsher sentence? Whenever he had questions about ECN's technology, he'd ask Jase. This was Ryno's opportunity to return all that help. He offered some tips on how to defeat the FSF firewall and asked:

= *What's so urgent about accessing ecn?*

Jase didn't respond.

Ryno opened a can of cider he'd squirreled away in his backpack. In the midst of this shitstorm, Jase's focus on his work was either impressive or delusional. Why did he need to urgently connect to ECN? Was Jase just addicted to watching ECN's high-speed baseball game? Did he want to learn something new? Or was he trying to cover up his tracks?

III

Part Three

26

Message

*Of all of our inventions
for mass communication,
pictures still speak the most
universally understood language.*
—Walt Disney

* * *

*next morning
day 13
2033 January 26*

* * *

Dan nodded in and out of sleep on the leather couch in his modern, glass-and-metal-clad office at Stanford. He'd slept fitfully last night, worrying about Lita and trying to contact Luke Johnson. He'd left multiple messages with Luke's digital avatar and his UT Austin office staff.

The ring of an incoming call jolted Dan awake. He stood to take the call at the screen on his standing desk. The screen switched to an image of Luke, sitting at his rustic desk in his pine-paneled office and wearing a saddle brown-colored, felt Stetson cowboy hat.

"Morning, bud. Got your messages," Luke said in his baritone Texas twang. "Been tryin' to contact your bride-to-be for the past twenty-four hours."

Dan rubbed his eyes. "Hey, Luke. Lita and her lab team are holed up under FBI protection. The death threats have been outrageous."

"That's a damn shame. Horseshit-crazy DOTEs are everywhere now, even here in Texas." Luke looked hard at Dan and flipped up his monocle on its rattlesnake leather frame. "Can you get a message to Lita confidentially?"

"Yeah. The team has a stealth comm channel. I'm on it too. An hour ago, I spoke with Lita. Her team's despondent, and she's distraught. Do you have something important to tell her, that'll give them hope?"

"Well, bud, I shouldn't be telling you this, on account of international protocols. But screw that. Lita's suffered enough. I'm gonna tell you something that'll change everythin'."

"Change everything?" Dan raised an eyebrow. "What do you mean?"

"You sit yourself down first."

Dan sat in his office chair, put up his feet on the adjacent coffee table, and crossed his arms. "All right, I'm sitting."

"About a month ago, we powered-on enhancements to our telescope orbitin' the moon. And several days ago, Lita asked me to use the telescope to take a close look at the Proxima system to see if we could detect any anomalous trajectories emerging, like a gravitational slingshot."

"Yep, Lita mentioned you in her Berkeley newspaper interview."

"I saw that interview. Those two students followed up with me. At that time, I had nothin' definitive to tell them."

Luke leaned into the screen. "But the day before, I had confidentially told Lita that we hadn't detected any strange trajectories. Instead, we'd observed something else strange when the moon periodically shielded our telescope from the sun and the sun's reflection off Earth. Coherent light in the ultraviolet spectrum is emanatin' from the atmosphere-less moon of Proxima b. You could call it an ultraviolet laser emission. That's different from a conventional laser emission which uses visible light, the kind human-made devices commonly generate."

Dan uncrossed his arms.

"But here's what we discovered after my conversation with Lita. Like a rotatin' twentieth-century lighthouse, the emission from the Proxima b moon sweeps across a large radius and periodically holds its focus on our moon. When it's focused on the moon, the emission becomes pulsed and its frequency methodically steps down to the microwave spectrum. Curiously, the change increases the emission's reflectance off the near side of the moon's mare—its relatively smooth surface area."

Dan raised his eyebrow again. "Interesting, but how does that change everything?"

"Stimulated microwave emissions have been observed from interstellar space. But the frequency step down and pulsing pattern led our team to hypothesize that this isn't a natural phenomenon. Somebody is generating this and wants us to see it. So, we used my lab's new microwave telescope to study the transmission bouncin' off the moon."

"You mean like laser-based moonvertising that was banned years ago?"

"Exactly, but at an unfathomable scale," Luke said. "In addition to its reflectivity, the transmission's attributes are optimal for pinpoint focus over an astronomical distance. I ain't shittin' you, it's impressive and way beyond our capabilities."

Dan took his feet off the table and leaned forward. "What did you find?"

"From our space telescope's position, when the moon is full relative to Proxima and new relative to our sun, the reflection reveals a hi-res sixty-one-second animation that repeats every sixty-seven seconds. Kinda like how old-style cathode ray TVs worked."

"Animation?" Dan said, his brows furrowed.

"Yes, and the animation's unmistakable. It shows our eight-planet solar system and the Proxima solar system on paths that fly by each other. Amazingly," Luke said with a raised voice, "an animated message to Earth is being projected from the Proxima b moon usin' our moon as a screen. This supports Lita's flyby discovery. More incredibly, it proves the existence of advanced extraterrestrials. These aliens probably inhabit Proxima b. They're certainly more advanced than us—because they've been aware of the flyby years before we discovered it. Also, they're capable of sendin' this sophisticated deep-space message. They're tryin' to tell us somethin' 'bout the flyby."

After a speechless moment, Dan jumped to his feet and yelled, "Luke, you need to immediately announce this discovery. It'll stop the death threats and allow Lita to come home."

"Dadgum it, wish I could. If not for Lita, we'd have never looked for and discovered this. But we can't announce this until it's corroborated. The international protocols regardin' the search for extraterrestrial intelligence require that I get verification from other research centers. We can't have a damn premature public disclosure before verification. Hell, I shouldn't have told you."

Dan's monocle flashed.

= *Source: Principle #2 of the Declaration of Principles Concerning the Conduct of the Search for Extraterrestrial Intelligence.*

"Our space telescope's unique. So I've discussed with several other observatories how they might detect the message with their technologies. Now that they know what to look for, it shouldn't take but a day to confirm our findings. I'm also fixin' to notify the US Space Force to confirm the transmission. So the government and DOTEs know this ain't some jackass academic elite bullcrap."

Dan rubbed his chin. "This does change everything, for Lita and humanity. Why an animation? Why not simply use the pulsing to send something like a Morse code?"

"Think about it, bud. How could we interpret an alien encoded message? Images are universal. At least for species that can see them. Fortunately, we have a telescope that can sense the images they sent."

"Got it. That's brilliant," Dan said. "Why an animation of the flyby?"

Luke shrugged. "Could be—"

"Wait," Dan said. "I can't think about that now. I need to tell Lita so she can stop tormenting herself."

After the call, Dan opened Ryno's communication channel. But the connection simply returned *FSF Block*. He stared at the letters in disbelief. The FSF must have discovered the hack—at the worst possible moment. Thrilled by Lita's vindication, but frustrated by his inability to tell her, he stood and paced with his head lowered.

How had the FSF found the hack? An hour before the call with Luke, Lita had used the connection to schedule a team discussion for noon. He had mentioned the network connection on his call with Luke. Was the FSF bugging his non-encrypted calls, or Luke's?

His throat tightened. He held in the spasm of a sob. A dry heave retched his head forward.

27

Surfing

*Scientists are surprised to discover
a massive gas cloud
near the Andromeda galaxy*
—NPR Morning Edition,
2023 January 19

* * *

*next morning
day 14*

* * *

With remnants of the morning fog fading, Dan surfed at San Francisco's Ocean Beach. He'd given up trying to sleep. Maybe surfing the cold ocean waves would take his mind off the tense situation. While paddling out for a second ride, the monocle in his ocean goggles flashed a d-message from Luke.

= *Alien message confirmed by az u. Tx chancellor informed. Press conference at 12 central. Trying to contact fbi & fsf so lita doesn't have to wait 4 hrs to be freed.*

Dan turned his board around and frantically paddled to shore. He paced along the beach with his wetsuit top unzipped and tried to contact the FSF officer and FBI Agent Leight. They didn't respond, and their offices couldn't find them. How odd. Were they already aware of Luke's discovery?

28

Knocks

> ...we misunderstand how we will
> probably someday discover intelligent life
> elsewhere in the universe.
> —Garrett Graff, Author of
> *UFO:*
> *The Inside Story of*
> *the US Government's*
> *Search for Alien Life*
> *Here—and Out There*
> as stated on NPR's Fresh Air interview
> 2023 November 27

* * *

an hour later

* * *

Sequestered in the frigid little house, Lita had the bed blanket pulled up to her chin and the tattered curtains drawn. Despite her exhaustion, she hadn't slept well. Losing Ryno's group comm channel had worsened an already grim situation.

Three knocks on the front door interrupted her ruminations.

"Professor Bloom, "a person said, her voice muffled by the door. "This .... FBI ..."

"What now?" Lita yelled, unable to hear everything the person at the door had said. Was the FBI here to officially charge her and take her into custody? How much worse could this get?

More muffled words came through the door. "... here to take you ..."

Lita wanted to yell *go away*. A howling wind ruffled the curtains on the open window to her side. Maybe she should squeeze through it. Go underground while proving her innocence.

Instead she summoned the energy to push off the covers and trudge to the door, still dressed in the sweatshirt and sweatpants she'd been wearing when her isolation nightmare started. The flimsy floorboards creaked under her.

She cracked open the door. "What do you want?"

"Professor Bloom, University of Texas has confirmed your flyby discovery," Agent Leight said with a tender smile. "I don't have the details yet. The FSF halted its investigation. I'm here to escort you home."

Lita fell to her knees and sobbed into her palms.

The agent knelt with her. She hugged and rocked Lita. "Your nightmare's over. Let's get you home."

* * *

KNOCKS

Jase sat at the little house's desk, still trying to break through the FSF firewall, when knocks at the front door interrupted him.

"Jase Park-Muller, I'm with the FBI. You've been exonerated. I'm here to take you home."

Jase folded his screen and grabbed his unopened suitcase. Motioning for Cogg to join him, he opened the door and said, "What took you so long to figure out the truth?" He didn't wait for, or expect, an answer from the FBI officer. He sat in the back seat of the officer's vehicle and waited to be driven home. He just wanted to get back to the ECN lab.

* * *

Marc slammed the cottage's front door shut and limped past the FBI officer without establishing eye contact or uttering a word. He wasn't sure this ordeal was over and his academic reputation would be restored. But at least he could go back to his wife. Hopefully, all this turmoil and his anxiety hadn't harmed her pregnancy.

And hopefully, he'd find a way to bring justice to the miscreants who caused this calamity. Evil should have consequences.

* * *

Ryno ran both his hands through his hair, screamed "wow-ser," and bear-hugged the FBI officer. The officer was too heavy to lift off the floor. While stuffing his few belongings into his backpack, Ryno yelled, "I'm riding shotgun on the drive home."

"Fine," the officer said and opened the vehicle's passenger side front door.

Ryno hopped into the seat, rolled down the window, and sang his favorite Sinatra song, "Fly me to the Moon."

He couldn't wait to tell Pari and for Pari to tell her father. Maybe he could be there to see her father's reaction. That'd be sweet.

29

Singularitive

> Finding extraterrestrial life would be
> "the single greatest discovery in history."
> —*Steven Hawking*
> as quoted in NationalGeographic.com
> 2018 May 2

* * *

noon central time on the same day
2033 January 27

* * *

With the Texas Tower behind him, the Texas State Capitol dome on the horizon in front of him, and a sea of hushed people before him on UT Austin's South Mall, Luke adjusted his signature cowboy hat and started the press conference.

"Ten days ago, researchers at University of California, Berkeley discovered that our solar system and the Proxima solar system are on galactic orbits that'll put the two systems within a half light-day from each other a hundred years from now. Misinformed rumors compelled the Berkeley lab team to announce the flyby prior to independent verification. However, before those rumors, their lab leader, Professor Lita Bloom, had asked me to focus my lab's space telescope at Proxima. Lita had a hunch that the unique capabilities of our telescope might detect the emerging trajectory of Proxima's slingshot if we specifically looked for the phenomenon."

Luke paused to take a gulp of ice water to soothe his cotton mouth and calm his trembling from the adrenaline-fueled anticipation that his announcement would change humanity forever.

"Our investigation, which I'll detail in an imminent publication, encompassed the entire Proxima solar system including its Goldilocks planet, Proxima b. Our analysis revealed a message to Earth. This message appears to be from advanced extraterrestrials on Proxima b. This morning, colleagues at the University of Arizona verified the message. The message references and thereby confirms the solar-system flyby discovery. Here it is."

Amidst lots of murmuring in the audience, Luke projected the animation on the wall-sized screen behind him and made it available to the public via the internet-S.

"Here and here," Luke said, making circles with his laser pointer, "y'all can see the unique details of our eight-planet solar system. Here are the rings of Saturn on the sixth planet. And here's Proxima Centauri's three-star system. It's unmistakable. Additionally, the animated message has two mysterious attributes. First, it shows what looks like an explosion on the surface of the planet Neptune. We don't know what that's intended to convey. Second, as the solar systems near each other, the message renders a dotted line between Proxima b and Earth. This line could indicate some kind of communication or possibly a visit between the inhabitants of the two planets."

A frenetic Q and A session followed. The last question was, "Professor Johnson, is the message a friendly greeting, a pragmatic notification, or an ominous warning?"

Luke shook his head. "Reckon I can't answer that yet. But we have several decades to figure it out."

Before the press conference ended, Luke returned to the stage during the UT chancellor's concluding remarks. "Apologies for interruptin', but I just received a notification that the US Space Force confirmed the existence of the alien moon message."

Only then did the audience respond with a standing ovation.

When he stepped offstage, Luke received a d-message from Dan.

= *Lita and lab team free. Thank u luke.*

30

More Discoveries

an hour later

* * *

After the FBI had returned Jase to his apartment, he scootered to the lab to access ECN. The FSF had not yet re-enabled network connectivity to the quantum computer.

Cogg galloped alongside, dodging fire hydrants, street flora, and other sidewalk obstacles. His pet's agility and its joyous facial expression warmed Jase's heart.

When Jase arrived at the lab, he scrutinized the latest ECN report. His eyes scrolled across the numbers, forming images in his mind. A now familiar pattern emerged. But in reverse. After a few seconds, he hugged Cogg and bumped his fist as he'd done at the protest fourteen days ago. "I knew we'd find something like this."

Cogg howled like a wolf at a full moon.

As ECN continued its analysis, it charted Proxima's path further into the future and back in time. The report revealed a second discovery. Jase d-messaged the team to come to the lab. They agreed to meet there in an hour.

He leaned back in his chair. The last time he'd felt this way was just after he'd read ECN's preliminary flyby report two weeks ago. Lots had happened since then. Would this discovery turn his life upside down again?

He turned to the window. Two students, holding hands, walked across the grassy quad. Could this discovery have implications for humanity and the planet? He didn't have the knowledge to fathom a hypothesis. That was something he now aspired to change.

* * *

The metal door of the ECN lab swung open. Jase looked up from his desk and stood. Ryno bounded toward him and bear-hugged him, lifting him off the ground. Jase pushed against Ryno's chest but couldn't weaken the hug.

Marc entered the lab and put his hand on Jase's shoulder. "Sorry for doubting you. Can you forgive me?"

Jase nodded and grinned at Cogg. Despite the apology, he still had a hard time keeping eye contact with Marc.

Ryno lifted his arms and partially bowed to Jase. "I'm in awe of your curiosity, your daring, tenacity, and humbleness. You're my role model."

Lita stood at the door. Ryno turned and hugged her. She shrieked with laughter.

"Enough with the accolades," Lita said, with a white, toothy smile. "You're embarrassing our maverick. Jase, you have something new to show us?"

"Indeed," Jase said, trying to ignore his déjà vu. "Ongoing ECN an-analysis has been charting Proxima's past trail through the galaxy. The report shows the three-star system's orbital physics are mind-bogglingly complex. Apparently the stellar gravitational slingshot has occurred intermittently, narrowing Proxima's elliptical orbit around the galaxy."

"What's it mean?" Ryno asked.

"It means that each slingshot brings Proxima in proximity to our solar system. Since we're rotating around the galaxy in the same direction, we've had flybys with Proxima as recently as two million years ago, fifty-five million years ago, and sixty-five million years ago. Check out the visualization of ECN's analysis."

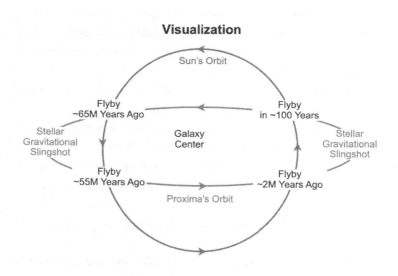

The team members watched the visualization. "Fascinating," Marc said. "This periodic interaction could mean that Centauri is actually a four-star system that includes our sun."

"Indeed, this could be a periodic physical cycle of our solar system," Jase said.

"But it seems like more of a disruptive cycle," Ryno said. "Not a stable one, like ocean tides."

Jase continued speculating with his lab mates until Lita interrupted. "I d-messaged university leaders. They're blown away by our new discovery, especially the flyby a mere two million years ago. We're scheduling a press conference for noon tomorrow. This time, we're anticipating that news of the discoveries will spread, future fast."

31

Sunset

sing-gu-lar-i-tive
siNGgyə'lerətēv/
noun
A scientific discovery,
technological development,
or social movement
that has an abrupt and profound
impact on humanity
(Derivation: **Singulari**ty + Declara**tive**)

* * *

early evening of the same day

* * *

When the video recording of Luke's moon message speech ended, Lita folded the screen and turned to Dan. "I'm still blown away by the alien message."

Nestled beside her in the two-seat Adirondack chair on their condo's concrete and glass balcony, Dan sipped from his glass of Australian shiraz. "Everyone's still gobsmacked. What an astounding two weeks we've had."

"What a day I've had," Lita said. "This morning I woke up in isolation barely able to get out of bed, worrying the FSF would arrest me and my lab team today."

"I wondered the same thing. Except I assumed your arrest would be on false pretense."

Serene for the first time in many days, Lita took a belly breath and inhaled the citrus scent from the two dwarf lemon trees in the balcony's planter boxes. She meditated as the setting sun reached the horizon of the ocean behind the Golden Gate Bridge.

Ringing from her handset interrupted her tranquility.

"It's from Shenzhen," she said. "I should probably answer it."

Dan shrugged.

"Professor Bloom?" Lita and Dan heard through the speaker.

"Yes."

"This is Amanda Chau, the executive director of the Consortium's Committee for the Advancement of Science and Technology. I'm thrilled to tell you that minutes ago the committee voted to award a Singularitive Prize to you and your Berkeley lab team, along with the Texas team."

"Wow," Lita said, "I'm speechless. That's amazing." She turned to Dan. "Wait, is this a joke?"

"It's no joke," the director said. "Launched in 2030, the Singularitive Prize is awarded for discoveries that have an abrupt and profound impact on humanity—in beneficial ways. We make the award soon after the discovery, not annually. So we ask that you and your co-winners be in Shenzhen three months from today to accept the prize and its one hundred million yuan in unrestricted funds."

Lita thanked the director and committed to traveling to Shenzhen for the ceremony. After giving Dan a big hug and wet kiss, she d-messaged her lab team.

Moments later, her handset buzzed with d-messages of congratulations, including a high five emoji from Luke in Texas.

As the sunset transitioned to the gloaming, Dan resumed the couple's discussion. "I'd like to trailblaze a new branch of xenology focused on the Proximans."

"That'd be fascinating. I can't wait to study the astrophysics of Proxima's slingshots."

Lita reached out for Dan's hand. "This is all happening so future fast. I wish my mom and dad were alive to see this."

He nodded and squeezed her hand.

"Thinking about my parents makes me want to start a family," she said. "It also makes me want to address the planet's societal problems, for future generations."

"I know you'd be a great mom. That itself is a contribution to the next generation. And I look forward to contributing as a great dad." He brought the back of her hand to his lips, kissed it, and pressed it against his warm cheek.

She unzipped the front of her blouse, straddled his hips, held his face, and kissed him. Dan soothed and inspired her. She wanted nothing more than to love him, conceive their child, and take on the world tomorrow.

32

More Announcements

next day
day 15

* * *

"Now it's my pleasure to introduce Singularitive Laureate, Professor Amelita Bloom," the UC Berkeley chancellor said after making a few opening remarks at the press conference held at the University Club on top of the campus' Memorial Stadium. The wide-open, floor-to-ceiling, sliding glass walls provided unobstructed views of the hills to the east and the San Francisco Bay to the west.

An explosion of applause and standing ovation greeted Lita as she walked on stage with her arms raised. At the lectern, she drank in the cheers, pointed, and smiled at the dozens of attendees who'd contributed to the flyby discovery.

As she scanned the crowd, she came upon Robert Bob along the back wall. He stood motionless, his face as blank as a rag doll's. She rolled her shoulders back and put her hands on her hips, but didn't give Bob the satisfaction of her obviously noticing him. She wasn't going to allow him to taint this moment of glory.

When the attendees took their seats, Lita highlighted her team's additional discovery that the Proxima solar system and Earth's solar system had been on galactic orbits in which they'd had intermittent flybys.

In the concluding remarks, Lita stiffened and urged the world to pursue a litany of unknowns. "How long have the aliens been sending the flyby message? Why send it, and, in particular, what's the meaning of the two mysterious attributes of the message? To what extent, if any"—she paused and smiled at Dan—"have the previous flybys impacted Earth? To what extent will the upcoming flyby and Earth's orbital tweak disrupt our planet?" Her smile faded and hands gripped the sides of the lectern. "Can we establish two-way communication with the aliens? How will the discovery of advanced alien life affect civilization?" She sighed. "Finally, if humans solve the biological challenges of deep-space travel, could we rendezvous with the aliens in the coming century? What will they be like?"

* * *

After the press conference, Lita and her team gathered on an adjacent outdoor deck to celebrate. "Why just seventy percent?" Lita said with a wry smile after Ryno showed her the online rating of the media event.

"According to the polls," Ryno said, "Lourdes Graham and her acolytes have convinced about a third of the Civ World the flyby and moon message are hoaxes."

"Nothing surprises me anymore," Benna said, tucking her hair behind her ears. "The apocalyptic group, The End of Earth Society, and its leader, Robert Bob, are returning to the campus. They're spreading their new belief that the dotted line in the message indicates the aliens will invade and conquer us."

Benna took a sip of champagne. "Get this, those doomsayers also claim it's ominous that the alien animation is precisely sixty-one seconds long and it repeats exactly every sixty-seven seconds—which are consecutive prime numbers. Bob thinks the aliens are spying on us. Otherwise how else would they know humanity's basic unit of time is a second? He also babbled something about how that pair of prime numbers has double sixes, and the seven minus the one equals a third six. Apparently three sixes are a *Bible* reference to the devil."

Lita chuckled. "That's just fantastical."

"It gets worse," Marc said, looking down at the floor as he read his monocle. "The US Space Force briefed the Congress. That caused a backlash from elected officials, like Congressman Foster. Foster and Lourdes Graham are continuing to discredit our discoveries. The two even demanded that NASA stop funding our Earth collision research."

Marc flipped up his monocle. "That seems vengeful in a way that hurts humanity, not just our lab."

Lita shook her head. "If you believe the *Bible* book of 'Revelations' End Times Armageddon prophecy is imminent and will be glorious, what's the point of identifying an Earth collision years from now?"

"I can't fathom that government leaders, who make decisions affecting our future, believe in End Times delusions," Jase said. "Ap-apocalyptic conspiracists are running the country."

Lita turned from her colleagues and scanned the East Bay

metropolis. "I'm with Benna. None of this surprises me. It's like in the early twenty-first century when many elected officials tried to discredit science and the scientists who warned about human-caused climate change."

"Interestingly," Jase said, "the basis for Congressman Foster's disbelief of the flyby is no longer blamed on ECN manipulation. Instead, he and his supporters simply doubt machine learning can foresee stellar gravitational slingshots and project solar-system trajectories a hundred years into the future."

Marc flipped down his monocle and continued summarizing the news feeds. "Meanwhile, parts of civil society like public education, pop culture, and the mass media are grappling with the implications of the discovery of advanced extraterrestrials. Though some polls show almost half the world doesn't believe it."

Benna pointed at her head. "Again, not surprised. Most people didn't believe Copernicus and Darwin."

Lita rubbed her chin and pursed her lips. "The world's baffling. And it's gonna get crazier before it gets better. If it gets better. Let's hope science and truth prevail."

33

Portend

six months later

* * *

Lita peeked out the open window from her makeshift dressing room at Chabot Space & Science Museum. Dozens of guests had gathered on a xeriscaped lawn at the center's observation deck perched on a scenic hilltop in Oakland, California. Herbs in a nearby garden scented the air. Insects buzzed around the lavender, and hummingbirds flitted among wisteria crawling up a trellis archway under which she would soon walk. Museums were like temples to her and Dan. So getting married at Chabot seemed fitting.

Dan and his best man stood to one side of the wedding's officiant. Lita's best woman, Benna, stood on the officiant's other side.

Just fifteen minutes behind schedule, Lita stepped out of the room and under the trellis across the lawn from where Dan stood. The crowd turned their attention to her and hushed. Her

3D-printed, silver-colored wedding dress reflected the sunlight and revealed her six-month pregnancy. She placed her hand on her belly to caress the kicking fetus inside. Her bioluminescent bracelet and ring shimmered.

Lebron joined Lita and accompanied her walk to Dan while Pachelbel's "Canon in D Major" played. Along the way, Lita smiled at Luke, Lain, Shelley, Jase and his cogg—sporting a black bow tie. Steps later she gave a little wave to Marc and his pregnant wife, holding hands, and another wave to Ryno and Pari, their arms looped around each other's waists. Ryno ran his hand through his hair and gestured a thumbs-up.

At the end of their ceremony, the officiant placed two wine glasses, each wrapped in a cloth towel, at Lita's and Dan's feet.

"The glass in this ancient ritual," the officiant said, "symbolizes that even in joyous times, we should keep in mind that our lives will hold sadness as well as joy, laughter and tears, along with growth and setbacks. The cloth around the glass represents the commitment that this couple and this community share to stand together through all the ups and downs of life."

When the officiant nodded, Lita and Dan stomped on the glasses while the guests cheered, "Mazel tov."

"I now pronounce you husband and wife," the officiant said.

Lita glanced at Ryno, who had repositioned himself in front of the audio controls for the museum deck's sound system. The guitar riff of "Beginnings" by Chicago started playing.

Lita and Dan embraced and held a deep kiss. For Lita, the glass-breaking ritual and music portended the things to come over the century that'll culminate in the Proxima flyby and Proximan encounter. This was only the beginning.

Note to Readers

The second novella in this series is available. For more information go to singularitive.com.

Your feedback is welcomed via a review on Amazon and Goodreads, email to singularitive@gmail.com, and the contact page of singularitive.com.